Praise for *The Typist*:

"Michael Knight tells the story of generals, war, and occupation through the eyes of a typist who proves himself to be the calm at the center of the storm. The result is this elegant, thoughtful, and resonant novel."
—Ann Patchett

"*The Typist* is Knight's best book yet. It reads with a combination of urgency and a quiet, rush-less path to the novel's slow reveal. There is not a misstep, not a mislaid sentence. I believed and breathed every single word. This book awed me." —Elizabeth Gilbert

"Elegant . . . Knight's novel is told in sparse prose, but the story has gravity and a heft that makes it a memorable read."
—Kristin Carlson, *Chicago Tribune*

"An understated, elegant, compact novel of the American occupation of Japan, by an underrated fiction writer."
—*California Chronicle* (Top 100 Books of the Year)

"Knight's prose is mercilessly understated and tight, as if mimicking contemporary Japanese masters like Abe or Oe. Add a touch of hopeless resignation in the face of tragedy—that echoes a Graham Greene protagonist—and Francis emerges as a classic, sympathetic non-hero with . . . a new, tenuous life to improvise." —*Oxford American*

"The narrator's strong first-person voice . . . gives the novel a pensive tone that has more in common with an Alice Munro story than a typical war novel. . . . With its spare, economical prose, this novel brings a different slant to the th

"I loved *The Typist*. It is a beautiful portrait of a kind of walking pneumonia of the spirit that seeks and finds its own cure. It is also, for me, most impressive because of its setting—in a time far before Knight ever drew breath. It is true imagining at its finest."

—Richard Bausch

"Packing sharp characterization and a roller-coaster plot into a brisk two hundred pages, *The Typist* is a notable feat of literary economy . . . [and its] brevity is a source of its power. . . . It is no small thing to convince a reader to suspend disbelief about well-known events; Knight does so masterfully." —*BookPage*

"Given the sin-rich atmosphere of *The Typist,* it may come as a surprise that the tone is more beatific than vulgar. But then Mr. Knight has never shied away from taking the unexpected angle in his fiction. . . . Knight's prose transforms even cheap booze and poor weather into lovely atmospheric touches. . . . [His] elegant prose recalls the fiction of W. G. Sebald, another author who explored the melancholy postwar consciousness with subtle mastery."

—*The Economist* (online)

"Knight paints a disquietingly dreamlike portrait of a postwar Japan . . . Not quite darkly comic, not quite ironic, Knight's book is driven by earnest, unaffected storytelling." —*Publishers Weekly*

"Knight cunningly details the confluence of the boredom of American soldiers and the economic plight of the post-bombing Japanese. Two cultures collide and gross exploitation occurs, but Knight is still able to craft heartfelt relationships amid the confusion."

—Blair Parsons, *Booklist*

The Typist

Also by Michael Knight

Divining Rod
Goodnight, Nobody
Dogfight and Other Stories
The Holiday Season

Michael Knight

The Typist

Grove Press
New York

"The Atom Bowl" first appeared in *Narrative* in November of 2010.

Printed in the United States of America
Published simultaneously in Canada

ISBN-13: 978-0-8021-4536-9

Grove Press
an imprint of Grove/Atlantic, Inc.
841 Broadway
New York, NY 10003

Distributed by Publishers Group West

www.groveatlantic.com

11 12 13 14 15   10 9 8 7 6 5 4 3 2 1

For my grandfathers—

Vernon DePauw Knight, Lieutenant Commander,
U.S. Naval Intelligence, who was on the beach when
General MacArthur returned to the Philippines.

and

Thomas Benton Bender, Staff Sergeant, U.S. Infantry,
who earned a pair of bronze stars for valor
on the battlefields of Europe.

Contents

The Atom Bowl

—Say your name.

—That's all right, Pawpaw. It doesn't have to be too official.

—Do it right. It's for school.

—My name is Daniel Vaughn and I'm a junior at Knoxville Christian Academy. That work?

—And say what it's for.

—American history. It's a history project.

—You should have me state my name, too. And tell the tape where the interview is being done and what day it is and all that.

—Pawpaw, this right here is why we don't come visit you more often.

—Just do it, boy. It's important.

—Please state your name.

—Martin Lanier Vaughn.

—It's three o'clock on Wednesday, September 10, 2010, and I'm here to interview my great-grandfather. This interview is being conducted at the Marble Hill Rest Home in Johnson City, Tennessee, where my great-grandfather is a resident. He is believed to be the last surviving participant of—

—You should call me Mister Vaughn on the tape. Or Ensign Vaughn.

—I'm not kidding, Pawpaw. If you keep it up, I'll interview Uncle Lemon.

—Go on then. If that's what you want. Some post-traumatic-stress sob story. But everybody's got an uncle was in Vietnam. I'm the last surviving participant of the fucking Atom Bowl.

The game was General MacArthur's idea. He imagined something inspiring, something symbolic. To this end, he chose Hiroshima for the site. Here occurred the single greatest act of destruction in the history of man, he said in one of many press releases on the subject, and now it will showcase man's infinite capacity for healing. Players were handpicked from among the troops in his command. This was the tag end of 1946. The military was rich in athletes. Uniforms were designed, equipment flown in from the states, the Marine Brass Band dispatched. A full company of engineers was assigned to shore up the old stone grandstand at what had been an equestrian center before the war, to build a scoreboard, goalposts. Local children were enlisted to crawl on their hands and knees, removing shards of glass and rubble from the field. If everything went according to plan, the Tokyo Giants would meet the Hiroshima Bears at precisely noon on New Year's Day, 1947, in The Atom Bowl—so dubbed by General MacArthur himself.

—What was it like?

—What was what like?

—Hiroshima.

—I can't describe it.

—Pawpaw, I swear—

—I'm not refusing to answer, dumbass. I mean to say it cannot be described.

—Try.

—It was horrible.

—Try harder.

—It was terrible.

—But what did it look like? What did you see?

—It looked like a fucking city that had a fucking atomic bomb dropped on it. That's what I saw.

That first night in Hiroshima, bedded down in brand new bunks in brand new Quonset huts, surrounded by the night sounds of near strangers, was a lonely and complicated one. They were tired from traveling. The wash of excitement over this unusual assignment was beginning to bleed away. They'd been allotted three cans of beer apiece at dinner and now they were thirsty and kept having to get up to piss. They'd all had ideas about the bomb but none of them was prepared for what they found. They pounded their pillows and twisted in their sheets. They barefooted to the latrine on concrete floors.

Michael Knight

—It was just us billeted on location. The Giants were up in Tokyo. See, the teams were divided between men assigned to units in and around Tokyo—that's where the occupation was concentrated—and men stationed in the provinces or at sea or anywhere else in the Pacific. I was on the *Bonhomme Richard*. How come you haven't asked me about all that? Before the game?

—I know the answers. You were a cook.

—But this is for the tape.

—It's a just research project, Papaw. It's not for a museum.

—You don't want to know about my service?

—Fine, Papaw—

—Ensign Vaughn.

—But Pawpaw—

—Or Mister Vaughn.

—Whatever. Ensign Vaughn, please tell me about your experiences in the navy before The Atom Bowl.

—I was a cook aboard the *Bonhomme Richard*. That's an Essex class aircraft carrier. Essex class means short hull. I bet it's hard to picture me in a ship's galley cause I'm so big but, buddy, I got so I could scoot around from the ovens to the boilers to the sink, my head ducked low to avoid the pipes and the fixtures. I was famous for my eggs.

Morning broke crisp and clear and they mustered on the field huffing little clouds of steam—among them Calvin Thomas, who'd been named MVP of the Rose Bowl not too many years before, and Y. A. Cole, who'd played wingback at Louisiana Tech, and Dante Pasquali, a second-string quarterback from Notre Dame. Equipment was divvied up. The smell of the leather helmets was reassuring. They hadn't worn cleats since college. The engineers were putting the finishing touches on the grandstand and there was something heartening in the noise they made, the necessary bang of restoration and renewal. It felt good to line up and stretch in neat rows, to run the old familiar drills. There were twenty-five of them, twenty-six if you included the lone negro, a buck private named Willie Wall. In the afternoon, they separated into groups. Calvin Thomas took the backs and ends, Marty Vaughn the lineman—big meat, he called them. He'd played left tackle at Tennessee. They practiced until dusk, sorting out who would play where, who would go both ways. When it was at last too dark to see the ball, they gathered at midfield and elected Calvin Thomas captain of the team. As a first lieutenant, he was the ranking officer in the bunch. And a number of the men remembered his performance in the Rose Bowl, remembered the reverence with which the radio announcer had intoned his name, remembered his gift for picking up yards after a catch. They adjourned to the showers and the mess, then sallied forth in search of panpan girls and *katsutori soku,* a local brew, four glasses of which rendered temporary blindness in the drinker.

*   *   *

—Two weeks. That's how much time they gave us to prepare. We didn't bother with a game plan or nothing. We figured Dante Pasquali could throw the ball to Calvin Thomas or hand the ball to Calvin Thomas or stand aside and let Calvin Thomas take the fucking snap. Mostly we just didn't give a shit. Word came down from Tokyo that we'd be facing Bill Bertelli . . . Bullet Bill? The fullback? You mean to tell me you never heard of Bullet Bill Bertelli?

—Nope.

—Holy Cross? All-American? Grantland Rice called him—

—Who?

—How much do your parents pay to send you to that so-called school?

—I have no idea.

—Do the Four Horseman of the Apocalypse ring a bell?

—Famine, Pestilence, et cetera. It's a Christian school, Pawpaw.

—No, goddamit, I'm talking about . . . Oh, nevermind. What I'm trying to tell you is it was just supposed to be an exhibition. Nobody took it serious. Bill Bertelli or not, we figured the Giants felt the same. I was happy to be on dry land for a while. Don't get me wrong. I loved the navy. And I'm proud of my service. It was the fucking navy won the Pacific. But a man my size, those boats get a little cramped after a while.

—What do you remember about the rest of the team?

—They were from all over. The newspapers made a big deal about how we represented however many states and all four branches of the service. Good men. The only one didn't fit was the nigger.

—Pawpaw.

—What? You don't like that word?

—Nobody likes that word.

—I said fuck not ten seconds ago you didn't flinch but I say nigger—

—It's different. Just talk about the game, ok.

—I was trying to, goddamit. What I was trying to tell you was most of us, the way we looked at it was like an extended leave. We didn't know what the brass expected. We thought we'd have us a good old time.

They found a place by the river that served a drinkable *katsutori soku*. Two of the original walls were intact but the other two were cobbled together with roofing tin and salvaged wood, some kind of putty in the seams. The planks of the floor were mismatched, the gaps between them wide enough that you could see through to the dusty, shadowy region down below, a kingdom of rats and spiders. A bare bulb dangled from the ceiling. Cold seeped in from everywhere. They tried to make sense of football for their hosts but their Japanese was too rudimentary and the English of the locals was even worse and there exists no translation for words like quarterback and touchdown. In crumbling side rooms if they were lucky and in the alley out back if they were not, panpan girls hiked their kimonos or went down on their knees. There was even one panpan girl with a withered hand willing to accommodate a negro but Willie Wall did not indulge. He lead his panpan girl into the alley and sat with her in the dark, hidden by a pile of rubble. They pitied each other in silence. To Willie Wall, the moon looked bigger in Japan and seemed always to be full. When enough time had passed, he returned her to her colleagues and poured himself a glass of *katsutori soku* and lied about the appalling things he'd made her do so that neither of them would be embarrassed.

—Turn off the tape.

—Why?

—Just do it, boy. Why you have to question every little thing?

—All right, Pawpaw, it's off.

—You a virgin?

—What?

—You heard me.

—That's none of your business.

—I'll take that as a yes. I want you to listen to me now. I know there aren't a lot of Nips in East Tennessee but do yourself a favor. Find one and fuck her. Take my word.

—I'll do that, Pawpaw. I'll start looking as soon as I leave here.

—You won't be sorry.

—While we're on the subject . . . I guess . . . why don't you tell me about the Japanese? Was there any resentment?

—Naw. After a while they even started coming around the field to watch us practice, men and women both. Kids, too. Lots of kids. They couldn't get over me, boy. They'd never seen a man so big. I may not be much to look at now but back then, I'm telling you, I was something. Six-foot-six. Two hundred sixty pounds. All of it muscle. I'd trimmed down a little since my college days. They'd point at me and giggle and hide their mouths behind their hands. There weren't no hard feelings.

—What about you? Did you ever feel guilty or anything?

—For what?

For Christmas, a patriotic poultry man in Oklahoma shipped three hundred live turkeys to Japan, several of which were diverted to Hiroshima and arrived at table that afternoon, dressed, of course, soaked all night in brine, burnished now and glistening from the ovens, somehow unruined by cooks whose talents ran more naturally to stew. The meal was supplemented by cranberry sauce canned in the states and rice grown in Japan and brown gravy, which the cooks had no trouble whipping up. Brown gravy was a specialty of the house. When the meal was finished, they lurched full-bellied into the street. The panpan girls were waiting. A little boy applauded as they passed. Overhead, the universe unfurled. A poet once wrote that the night sky is the nearest thing in nature to human emotion and he was right, as poets sometimes are.

—I'm serious. I want to know what you think I should feel guilty for.

—Nothing. Forget I asked.

—Let me tell you something. We didn't start that war. That's on the Japs. We didn't give the order to drop the bomb either. But thank God somebody did. Or half of us wouldn't of been there to fool around with something like The Atom Bowl. Most of those men had been in the mess up to their necks. Half of them had Purple Hearts. You may not have heard of Grantland Rice or Bullet Bill Bertelli but I know you've heard of kamikazes. Well, boy, I have looked upon those crazy fuckers with my own eyes. We'd earned the right not to feel guilty about nothing.

Christmas night, the temperature dropped fifteen degrees. A cold front moved in while they slept. The morning sky was like an old white bowl turned upside down. The press had been trickling in since dawn, reporters from every newspaper in Japan and Americans in their fedoras and Europeans who smoked brown cigarettes and dressed, despite the cold, like they were on safari. It occurred to the Hiroshima Bears that perhaps they had underestimated the gravity of the occasion. Perhaps they should have been taking The Atom Bowl more seriously. Perhaps something was at stake. The nature of that something was uncertain but they could feel the weight of it as they practiced. The ball was frozen, hard as marble, impossible to catch. Their feet felt clumsy and mis-sized. They suffered every block and tackle in their bones. Near the end of practice, Marty Vaughn tripped Willie Wall for no good reason. Vaughn was shivering, exhausted. He was embarrassed by how he'd played before the press. He had a hangover for the ages. Willie Wall bounced up off the ground, a blur of fists and knees, teeth and elbows. In the few long seconds that passed before Calvin Thomas remembered he was captain of the team, before he roused his players into action, Willie Wall broke Marty Vaughn's nose and jaw, cracked five ribs. Six corpsmen were required to remove Vaughn from the field.

Surely, somebody said, the situation in Tokyo was just as bad, but a reporter from *The Sporting News* informed them that General MacArthur, a lover of the game, often abandoned his office for hours to watch the Giants practice and they'd been compelled to whip themselves into shape. They'd knuckled down, focused on the fundamentals. They'd plotted and schemed. They look like pros, the reporter said. Now Marty Vaughn was in the hospital and Willie Wall was locked-up in the stockade. The guards agreed to release him once he cooled off but Willie Wall refused. He covered his face with a pillow and would not speak.

—It's just weird. The whole thing is weird. A football game played in the place where all those people died. You must have—

—If I could get up out of this wheelchair, I'd wring your neck.

—Don't be like that, Pawpaw.

—Ensign Vaughn.

—I'm not gonna call you Ensign Vaughn. You're my great-grandfather.

—And you're a walking talking argument for mandatory military service.

—Mom said this was a bad idea.

—Let me ask you a question about your mother: does she or does she not have fake knobs?

—I wouldn't know.

—Then let me ask another: are you a queer?

—Fuck you, Pawpaw.

—Ensign Vaughn.

—Fuck you, Ensign Vaughn. I'm done. I'll tell Uncle Lemon you said hello.

Unbeknownst to the participants, General MacArthur had arranged a series of express trains for the purpose of shuttling GIs to the Atom Bowl. He encouraged his officers to reward their men with passes. He wanted to be sure there was a crowd, plenty of witnesses. He wanted the bleachers brimming and rowdy in the newsreels. The first train, the one bearing the Tokyo Giants, pulled in on New Year's Eve and they kept coming through the night. By the time the players reported for the game, the stadium was full of spectators, all of whom had been carousing since they arrived.

MacArthur himself couldn't have contrived a more photogenic scene. It had started snowing at some point in the morning and the world looked dusted with confectioner's sugar. In the distance, behind the grandstand, rose the skeletal dome of Industrial Promotion Hall, all blackened beams and girders but down on the field the players were jogging in place and passing the ball around, an honest-to-God pregame warm-up. A fair number of locals had assembled in the open spaces beyond either end zone, their heads bowed in uneven rows against the cold like dark poppies in a winter field. The Marine Brass Band played John Phillip Sousa as MacArthur made his entrance at the gate, surrounded by officers, dignitaries, the whole entourage ringed with MPs, MacArthur in the middle of it all with his pipe clenched between his teeth.

His speech was later reprinted in half the newspapers in the world: I address you today on behalf of those voices forever silenced in the jungles and on the beaches and in the deep waters of the Pacific and on behalf of the thousands upon thousands who perished in an instant in this place. Make no mistake that a terrible thing happened here—at once the pinnacle of man's intellectual achievement and his capacity for self-annihilation. The forces of democracy were called upon to make an appalling choice but in making that choice obliterated the edifice of tyranny, leaving the world unshadowed, the sun no longer dimmed by oppression. Together, we celebrate not only the dawning of a new year but of a new world, a world whose limits will be as broad as the spirit and the imagination of man himself. I thank merciful God for giving us the courage to achieve victory and for turning our minds toward lasting peace. I ask Him to watch over those who take the field today, to keep them safe from injury and to grace this remarkable event with his presence. We all know the Lord loves football. I expect he's found himself a seat. If not, somebody please make room.

Then he saluted and a cheer leaped up from the stands and the players trotted out and suddenly the ball was in the air, the Giants kicking to the Bears in the city of Hiroshima, on the island of Honshu, in the occupied nation of Japan.

—Wait now. Wait. Please. Just wait one second before you turn that off.

—What is it?

—Nothing.

—If you've got something else to say, you might as well go ahead.

—You make Uncle Lemon tell the truth.

—Don't worry, Pawpaw. I won't put anything about government conspiracies in my paper.

—I'm not talking about all that.

—Then what are you talking about?

—Nothing. You wouldn't understand.

—Tell me.

—Just send that nurse over when you go.

The Atom Bowl was ugly from the start. Tokyo jumped out to the lead behind the running of Bill Bertelli. He lowered his shoulder and beat a path through the snow. He left a trail of bodies in his wake. On offense, without Marty Vaughn, Hiroshima couldn't stem the pass rush and Dante Pasquali didn't have time to look downfield for Calvin Thomas. He was sacked and sacked again. By the end of the first quarter, the Bears were trailing 14–0. General MacArthur scowled, his pipe jutting from the corner of his mouth like a sarcastic remark. The crowd was drunk, cold. They'd traveled all this way to see a football game, not a slaughter. The air rang with hoots and catcalls. The bleachers trembled beneath their feet. The locals looked on with equal parts dread and fascination. Marty Vaughn could hear the ruckus from his hospital bed, his jaw still wired shut. Outside, bits of gristle and scraps of paper ticked along the empty streets as if born along by the roar of the crowd. Panpan girls braced themselves for a post-game rush. Willie Wall was the sole occupant of the stockade. The guards wouldn't quit complaining that he'd made them miss the game but he ignored them. He sat on the floor with his back against the wall. From that distance, the crowd noise was muffled but persistent, like the steady murmur of rain.

Early in the second quarter, to everyone's surprise, the Bears scored when Calvin Thomas took the ball on a reverse and raced fifty-some yards untouched, the effort of which left him sidelined for three plays while he vomited into a bucket. They scored again two possessions later on a long pass from Dante Pasquali, who fled the pocket in terror and heaved the ball blindly into a scrum of players in the end zone, where it was batted up like a balloon and dropped into the arms of Y. A. Cole.

At halftime, the Bears collapsed around a barrel fire near the bench. They watched as the Marine Brass Band marched to "On Wisconsin"—General MacArthur's favorite fight song. The score was tied. They'd managed to stave off humiliation for two whole quarters. It didn't much matter what happened next. They could retain a modicum of dignity even if the Giants buried them in the second half.

Then, when the Marine Bass Band was finished, a chorus of local children tramped out to midfield, lead by a young woman in a patched black coat. She organized the children in two rows according to height and facing the grandstand. She darted her hands up and down and up again like birds and the children began to sing "God Bless America." In English. Maybe twenty of them, more girls than boys, but they were young enough that their voices had no gender. The sound of them was so sweet, so high and awkward and pure. At first the song was impossibly small against the hubbub of the crowd but they kept on singing, their voices building, gathering strength, and as they launched into the chorus, people were beginning to pay attention. *From the mountains, to the prairies, to the oceans, white with foam.* On the sideline, beside the smoking barrel fire, the Hiroshima Bears were quiet. Snow wisped down and melted in their hair. They gazed at the young woman and listened to the children and they were moved. Despite their fatigue. Despite their desire to be done with The Atom Bowl. *God bless America, my home sweet home.* They would have wept at the irony and beauty of it if not for pride. At the hospital, Marty Vaughn did, in fact, allow himself to weep because only nurses were there to see him and they bunched around his bed to rub his shoulders and hold his hands. Panpan girls all over town paused, lit cigarettes halfway to their lips. In the stockade, Willie Wall gripped the bars of his cell and told the guards he was ready to be released. I want to play, he said, and the guards hustled to comply. The song lasted no more than two minutes but in that time the Hiroshima Bears remembered the warm kitchens of their boyhoods and cold sea spray misting over the gunnels of landing craft. They imagined the far off droning of a plane. They pictured, to a man, the cloud billowing over the city, expanding, breathing, blazing, rendering everything unto dust. And as the last note faded, they burned at the knowledge of their own weakness. Kids, somebody said. They waited for the children to clear the field, then groaned and heaved themselves up and headed out to finish what they'd started, not restored exactly, not confident, but determined to make the rest of the game a war.

The Typist

I

After Pearl Harbor, my father was gone more often than he was home, piloting his tugboat from Mobile, Alabama, where we lived, to factories as far away as Louisville and Kansas City, barges riding low in the water from the weight of materials for the war effort. He'd been too young for the first war and now he was too old, but I was proud of him just the same.

For her part, my mother never seemed to mind the erratic schedule or to resent the other wives in our neighborhood, the ones whose husbands came home each night in time for supper, and though I admired my father very much, though I wanted to pilot a tugboat of my own one day, I minded on her behalf. When he wasn't on the water, my mother fussed over him, cobbling his favorite meals together, despite the rations, rubbing his feet while he read the paper, wearing her hair the way he liked, pressing a finger to her lips to make sure I didn't wake him in the morning. Then, in what seemed no time at all, my father would pack his grip and vanish from our lives again, the only proof of his existence dry whiskers in the sink and an extra pillow on my mother's bed.

My mother had been a secretary before she married, and during the war, she took piecemeal work for extra money, mostly papers for students at the Jesuit college in our town. Nights, she'd set her typewriter, a 1938 Corona Portable, on the kitchen table after dinner, and I'd linger over the dishes as a pretext to watch her. My mother was pretty all the time but her face in concentration was mesmerizing, lips pursed, eyebrows knitted. Her fingers flashed over the keys. It was my mother who taught me how to type. The trick, she told me, was to forget about your hands. I allowed these lessons only on nights when my father was away. She gave me scripture to practice on. *Blessed are the poor of spirit* and *For now we see through a glass darkly* and so forth. She was not an overtly religious woman—I never saw her cross herself outside of mass—but we attended services every Sunday, sometimes with my father, sometimes not, depending on his work schedule and his mood, and though I quit church in the army, I never did manage to shake what I would call a spiritual inclination.

Every so often, when my father was gone and my mother was lonely and sleep eluded her, she'd slip down the hall to my room and ask me to scoot over on my bed. I'd sigh and grumble out of a kind of teenage sense of obligation, but the truth is I didn't mind. She'd curl up with her chest against my back, her knees in the crooks of mine, her hands pressed together, as if in prayer, between my shoulders.

Our secrets: my typing lessons and her nights in my bed.

Looked back on, those days seem happy enough, all things considered. I had plenty of friends and I chased my share of girls without success. Before the war, the biggest thing to happen in my life was when Alabama whipped Stanford in the Rose Bowl. That was part of the problem, I suppose. I enlisted three days after graduation. Did my basic at Fort Benning. Got married two weeks before I shipped overseas. She was seventeen years old, one of those girls who made bandages for the Red Cross and danced with soldiers at the USO, and I was one of those soldiers headed off to war. Near the end of basic training, an assignments officer asked if I had any special talents. At first I could think of nothing, and we just kept looking at each other. Finally, I remembered I could type. I shipped out eighteen months before we dropped the bomb, my life so far receding, my life to come spreading out before me big as the ocean. I was attached to the Officers Personnel Section, a sort of military secretarial pool, of General MacArthur's headquarters, first in Brisbane, then Manila. In September 1945, a month after the surrender, the whole operation was relocated to Tokyo, where the story that I want to tell begins.

II

The Imperial Finance Ministry was converted into barracks for obvious reasons: it was big enough to serve the purpose, it had survived the bombing intact, and it was one of the few remaining buildings in Tokyo where the steam heat still worked. Billets were divided between general operations personnel, typists like myself, cooks, mechanics, and so on, and members of MacArthur's Honor Guard. By an accident of mathematics —an odd number of troops assigned to the clerical staff—I was bunked with an Honor Guard corporal named Clifford Price.

The Honor Guard was mustered before we left Manila. General MacArthur issued a directive to the commanders of all the combat divisions in the Pacific; I typed the orders up myself. Each division was to supply ten "distinguished" soldiers for reassignment to the Philippines, where they would serve as a personal escort for MacArthur and visiting dignitaries and the like. The criteria were strict: All members of the Honor Guard must have scored 110 or better on the General Classifications Test, must have a "sterling" combat service record, must be of "exemplary physique" and between five feet ten and six feet two inches tall. This last was so all their heads would be at more or less the same level on parade.

Honor Guard Company was among the first to enter Japan, so Clifford had moved into our room a week before I arrived. I found him sitting on the foot of his bed, right leg crossed over left, paring his toenails with a pocketknife. The room was neat enough and the walls were bare but already the room felt lived in, Clifford's watch and loose change on the desk, his odor in the air—feet and laundry and a powdery smell I couldn't name. Toenail trimmings on the floor. He took me in, then returned his attention to his foot.

"What's in the case?" he said.

Beyond the window, the world was dim with evening and I'd been on one plane or another since dawn and my ears were ringing and my mind was wiped blank from the shuffle and disorder of relocation. I'd forgotten that I was clutching a typewriter, still in its cardboard case, against my chest as if I intended to use it to keep my new roommate at bay. My CO, Captain Embry, had told me to leave the typewriter in Manila, said the army would have a new one waiting for me in Japan, but it was the most beautiful piece of machinery I'd ever seen, a 1942 Royal Super Speed, so black it negated light, round silver keys rising from the space bar in four tiers, 48 tiny platters perched on the fingertips of 48 tiny butlers, each letter offered up like something rare. Because I was good at my job, I'd been granted permission to keep the Super Speed in my quarters. I hoped, secretly, to take it with me when I shipped home.

"Typewriter," I said.

"You think you could do a letter for me?" Clifford said. "My mother always bitches that my handwriting is a mess."

"All right," I said.

"I told her if she kept complaining I'd quit writing period, but she knows it's a bluff. Bunny makes us write home once a week."

Bunny was my personal favorite among the nicknames the men had for MacArthur. I liked its obscurity—in two years under his command I'd never been able to find a single soldier who could explain its origins—and its versatility. It could serve as a term of affection or admiration or derision, with only the slightest variation in context and tone of voice.

I moved to set the Super Speed on what would be my bed but Clifford hopped up before I could and swiped his things off the desk.

"Put it here," he said, and so I did.

He dragged a footlocker out from under his bed, removed a notepad from atop a stack of neatly folded undershirts. He flipped pages until he found what he was looking for.

"He makes you write?" I said.

Clifford nodded. "To set an example for the regular army slobs. No offense. It's not bad. Bunny jumps us through a lot of hoops, but I was attached to First Cavalry before I got recommended. This is better by a longshot."

He handed me the pad, tapped the page.

"Can I type it later?" I said. "I'm beat."

"Sure," he said. "Whenever. As long as it's ready for the mail by Friday." He sat on his bed to sprinkle his feet with powder from a tube printed with Japanese letters.

"You play Ping-Pong?" he said. "They got tables downstairs."

He pulled on his socks and shoes.

"I'm beat," I said again.

"What's your name?"

I told him and he told me his and we shook hands.

When he turned to leave, I said, "You mind cleaning up your toenails before you go?" He stared at me for a second, then smiled in a way that made me wish I hadn't asked, policed his nail trimmings, stowed them in his breast pocket, and left me in possession of the room. For a minute, I just stood there, embarrassed, disoriented. Eventually, I made my bed and unpacked my duffel. At the bottom, tucked into a pair of blue civilian socks, was my wedding band. I'd quit wearing it my first week on active duty. I buried the socks at the bottom of my footlocker and stretched out atop the blankets on my bed. Without meaning to, I dozed off, woke up hungry a few hours later to the sound of Clifford snoring and, behind that, faintly, the patter of light rain.

Those first few months in Japan were my favorite of the war. There was plenty to be done, of course, especially for a typist, more work in some ways in the management of peace than in the prosecution of hostilities, but a shadow had lifted clear. I'll admit that I was fond of army life from the beginning, its regularity and routine, its absolute remove from the life I'd left behind. In Australia and then the Philippines, after Bunny retook Bataan, I'd abandoned myself to the steady, useful progress of the days, but always the possibility existed that something awful would pass across my desk. Even the good news—another island liberated, a successful bombing raid—was tinged with death. Now all that was over with. Bunny made it clear from the beginning that the Japanese were to be treated with respect, that it was their job to rebuild the country, not ours, that we were here to help, when help was wanted, and when it wasn't, we were to stay out of the way. Despite all the military trappings, we were basically spectators, civilians in army dress, watching while a nation reinvented itself according to Bunny's imagination.

Each morning, I woke at 0700, made my bed, showered, shaved, downed a cup of coffee and crossed Hibiya Park on foot to the Dai Ichi Sogo building, nodding at the locals and saluting as necessary to passing officers. My route took me alongside the Imperial Palace moat. Swans, pale as ghosts, gliding on the water. A pretty wooden bridge. A gatehouse and a stone wall on the other side. You couldn't see the palace itself. The grounds were too extensive, acres and acres of landscaping right in the middle of downtown Tokyo. The only people allowed across the moat were the Emperor and his staff. Even Bunny sent messages via special envoy. He could have changed the rules, but he believed that if he wanted to win over the locals it was important to treat their traditions and institutions with respect.

From 0800 to 1700, I typed whatever the brass needed me to type. The paperwork was endless, and I learned to type without reading at all, to let information pass directly from my eyes to my fingers without registering in my conscious mind, and this did wonders for my speed and precision. Now and then, especially if I was typing something from Bunny, a word or phrase caught my eye and I'd slow down enough to take in the meaning, but mostly I gave myself up to mindlessness. The act was a kind of self-hypnosis, I suppose. That's how it felt, anyhow. Most days, the hours passed in a tedious dream, and when the work was finished I could hardly remember a single thing that had crossed my desk. I strolled back through the park like a man who has just been roused from a slightly-too-long nap.

Walk a mile in any direction and you ran onto acres of devastation, heaps of rubble and rusted metal, old men and young boys sorting the debris for whatever might be salvageable and loading the rest into trucks to be carted off who knows where. If the wind shifted just right, everything smelled like wet ash. After our B-29s had taken care of all the industrial targets and still Japan had not surrendered, the air force ceased to discriminate, but by a stroke of pure good luck, the park and the financial district surrounding it, a few square miles altogether, were mostly spared. That's where we moved in—Little America, the locals called it. There was always a crowd gaping in through the windows of the PX at the shelves of canned goods and clothes and souvenir kimonos. "Demokrashi good," they'd say, when you emerged. "Demokrashi OK." They'd laugh and tug at your sleeve, and maybe you'd let them have your loose change. It should have been a sad sight but there was no rancor in it, not from either side. I felt decent and important and part of something bigger than myself. Bunny had set the tone. We weren't conquering these people, we were liberating them from centuries of tyranny. All of us were dimly aware that there were families living under railroad trestles somewhere in the city and that, because of food shortages, a letter from Bunny himself demanding that the War Department "send me more bread or send me more bullets" had passed through the Officers Personnel Section, but none of that was our fault, the way we saw it, and it was hard to keep those things in mind at all when Emperor Hirohito was posing for photos in Bunny's living room and the cherry trees in Hibiya Park looked exactly as they must have looked before the war and Little America was strung with Christmas lights in December and there were wreaths on all the lampposts and even the local entrepreneurs were selling holiday cards, woodcut prints of snowy mountains and brushy pines, the scenes beautiful and quiet, austere by comparison to the cards you bought back home.

Michael Knight

*　*　*

A story went around not long after we got settled in. Apparently, Bunny was on his way home from the office one night when he spotted a GI in an alley getting a handjob from a panpan girl. "You see that?" he said. "They keep trying to get me to put a stop to all this Madam Butterflying around, but I won't do it. My father told me never give an order unless I was certain it would be carried out." Clifford claimed to have the details direct from Bunny's driver. I don't know if the story or its source is true, but I know Clifford took it to heart. During the day he escorted Bunny from his quarters at the embassy to his office in the Dai Ichi Sogo building—just two floors up from mine— or he stood guard outside the building while Bunny was at work, or he paraded with the rest of the Honor Guard for visiting heads of state, but after hours he devoted himself to getting laid.

Not a particularly challenging endeavor. With the financial backing of what was left of the government, a group of Japanese businessmen calling themselves the Recreation and Amusement Association hired thousands of young women to provide "comfort" for the occupation forces. They issued a public statement, in English, within a week of our arrival: "We hope to promote mutual understanding between our conquerors and our people, to smooth the development of diplomacy and to abet the construction of a peaceful world." The whole business seemed remarkably open-minded and hospitable. Eventually, under pressure from Washington, Bunny nudged the Japs to outlaw state sponsored prostitution, but the ban didn't do much to slow the trade. Those girls had to make a living somehow, so they hired out to private houses or plied their wares in Ueno Station or in the Yurakucho district on the edge of downtown. It was so easy to get laid even Clifford got bored with hookers after a while.

He came into our room one night while I was knocking out a letter to my wife and flopped back on his bed. He didn't speak so I kept typing. I tried to write her once a month or so. Enough that I didn't feel guilty. After a few seconds, Clifford started sighing and cracking his knuckles loud enough for me to hear.

"What?" I said.

"Nothing."

"You need me to type something?"

"No," he said.

I went back to my letter. I'd hardly typed three words before he interrupted.

"How come you never go to panpan girls?"

My fingers hung over the home row.

"I'm married," I said, without turning around.

The springs squeaked as Clifford sat up on his bed.

"You're shitting me?" he said. "But you don't wear a ring. Do you? I never seen one. And you don't have any pictures. Have you been hiding pictures of your girl?"

"That's my business."

"It's weird is what it is," he said. "Besides, I know lots of married guys who get a little something now and then. No harm in it. Nobody'll ever know."

I yanked the letter out, balled it up, and tossed it toward the wastebasket. Missed. Clifford picked it up and for an instant I was afraid he'd read what I had written, the usual catalog of weather and routine, but he just dropped it in.

"What do you do?" he said. "You jerk off? Are you in here jerking off all the time when I'm not looking? You better not be. If my feet start sticking to the floor, we're gonna have words."

He was just messing around. He whopped me with his pillow. Then, suddenly, his expression went serious, almost sad.

"Well, I'm jealous," he said. "I truly am."

I admired Clifford in certain ways. Not just for his service record. He had a wide gullible face, like a boy swelled too fast to man-size, that belied a knack, even in peacetime, for putting himself in the middle of the action. He knew a guy in the motor pool who'd let him commandeer a jeep sometimes for late night rendezvous. Within weeks, he had worked out an arrangement where he purchased American products—tinned food, powdered milk, nylons, liquor, whatever—from the PX, then doubled his money reselling them to some shadowy connection on the Tokyo black market, called the *yami-ichi* by the locals. It was Clifford who found a houseboy named Eguchi to clean the barracks on our floor and convinced the rest of us to chip in. When he wanted something from you, this mix of innocence and savvy was difficult to resist.

We weren't pals exactly, but after a few months in close quarters we were comfortable enough, familiar enough, that it was possible to mistake us for real friends. I knew, for example, that the letters he wrote to his mother were ironic and affectionate and kind. I knew he was from Baltimore and he had a partisan view of his hometown. After a day trip to Kamakura, he pronounced that the coast of Japan couldn't hold a candle to the Eastern Shore. And I learned, on one of the rare nights he failed to organize an excursion, that Clifford was embarrassed to have come through the war unscathed. Most of the other members of the Honor Guard could boast of Purple Hearts. He told me this, I suppose, along with the requisite combat horror stories, both to impress me and because he had no one else to tell. If I happened to be around while he was preparing for an evening out, wet-combing his hair, splashing on aftershave, powdering his feet—he swore by the local powder he'd discovered—he always invited me to tag along, though it was understood that the invitation was a courtesy and I was expected to decline.

That's why it came as such a surprise when he cornered me in the rec room one evening and insisted that I join him on a double date. The room was low-ceilinged, hazy with smoke.

Ping-Pong and pool tables were set up in the back. The sound of the balls filled the air—the quick hollow taps of Ping-Pong, like clucking tongues, and the more substantial crack of pool. I was nursing a cup of coffee and paging through an old copy of *Life*.

"I need your help," he said.

Turned out he'd met a girl, the houseboy's cousin. She modeled for a department store in the Ginza shopping district during the day and worked as a hostess in a dance hall at night. *Nice girl,* Eguchi told him. *Very beautiful. Lives with family. Not panpan.* Her name was Namiki.

"She won't see me alone," Clifford said.

He'd been hesitant at first. Eguchi was maybe thirteen, always hustling. His hair had been shaved to stubble for delousing and he kept it like that, accenting an egg-shaped skull. He smoked a pack a day and called everybody Major, regardless of their rank. He did a bang-up job on the barracks but all of us understood his motives: Yankee dollars. He had a crew of younger kids working for him. He'd set them up in jobs like his or turn them loose to panhandle around Little America or send them out into the ruined suburbs to pick through the rubble for anything that might be resold. In every case, he took a cut of what they brought in. Even so, Clifford hadn't been able to resist following him to the department store where his cousin worked. She was right there in the front window. Hands on her hips. Chin up. One foot forward. A living mannequin—

perfectly, magically still. They stood there for a long time watching her. Then she shifted so that her hips were cocked, her left arm raised and bent at the wrist, as if to draw attention to something hovering in the air beside her head. Clifford made up his mind to find her at the dance hall that night.

He said, "She won't see me at all unless I bring somebody for her friend."

I'd been in the Oasis once or twice. It was tucked down in a basement on the Ginza. The beer was cheap and they usually had a band and it was nice, married or not, to hold a woman in your arms for a few minutes. These were mostly decent girls, poor but proper. The way it worked was you bought tickets for ten cents apiece from a cashier and then traded the tickets in to the hostess of your choice, ten tickets for a dance. Clifford spent twenty dollars dancing with Namiki. He kept her busy most of the night, had to fend off dozens of interested GIs. He asked her to see him outside the dance hall, let him take her on a real date, but she refused. Not even Eguchi's recommendation could change her mind. Finally, when it looked like a fight might break out between Clifford and a marine who'd been waiting for a turn with Namiki, she agreed to see him. On two conditions: the date had to take place during the day and Clifford had to find a companion for her friend.

"I guess she wants a chaperone," he said.

I closed the magazine, tossed it on the table.

"I can't," I said.

"I'm not asking you to fuck her. All you have to do is keep her busy."

"Ask somebody else."

"Look," he said. "I need to bring somebody nice, all right? I need to be sure that whoever I bring doesn't try anything with Namiki's friend."

He was sitting on the edge of the table, leaning forward over his knees as if he wanted to reach out and grab me and it took all his willpower to hold back.

We met the girls outside the department store where Namiki worked. This was March and you could still taste winter in the air, but it was warm enough that we didn't need our heavy coats. The Ginza had been a little beaten up in the air raids but nothing serious. Some of the buildings had burn scars, and here and there a window had yet to be replaced, but already most of the debris had been cleared away. The shops were open and bustling again. The sidewalk was lined with vendors selling bamboo mats and firecrackers and tobacco pipes made from machine gun cartridges. The sky was painted with wisps of cloud, and the street was thick with bicycles and old men pulling rickshaws and those odd coal-burning Japanese cars, belching black smoke. Most of the pedestrians were Japanese, but there were enough white faces that you didn't feel out of place, officers' wives with their retainers and GIs in bunches picking out presents for folks back in the States.

Clifford rubbed his hands together as we approached.

"Here we go," he said.

It was easy to see what he liked about Namiki. Big dimples, little nose. She was wearing a traditional kimono, sash wrapped and wrapped around her waist, silver leaves threaded into the silk, but her hair was held back by a white western-style head-band, likely a gift from one the men she'd danced with at the Oasis. The headband exposed a pale forehead and a perfect widow's peak. My girl was wearing a kimono too, but it was of the more casual variety. Blue cotton, unembellished. The locals had kimonos for all occasions. The hem fell to the middle of her shins and I could see, beneath her gown, what looked like men's wool socks and clogs. Her name was Fumiko, and when Clifford introduced us she bowed just slightly, keeping her hands tucked into her sleeves.

For the next two hours, we window-shopped. Clifford linked Namiki's arm in his and steered her along the sidewalk far enough ahead of us that I couldn't hear what he was saying. It was clear he wanted privacy, so if he and Namiki paused to look at something, I paused too, always maintaining the same distance as if in obedience to some archaic custom. Fumiko and I would stare without interest at whatever was before our eyes—porcelain dolls, pots and pans recast from army helmets—then move on when Clifford and Namiki were ready. Fumiko never once took her hands out of her sleeves, and when I asked questions in my phrasebook Japanese, she answered yes or no in English or said nothing at all. Here is what I learned about her: she had been a student before the war, but now she helped her mother run a vegetable stand in the Denechofu neighborhood. Here is what she learned about me: nothing. In two hours, she asked not a single question. I was bored in a hurry and angry at Clifford for dragging me along and angry at myself for being such a pushover. I was so embarrassed I could hardly look at her but I studied her reflection whenever we stopped at a window. At first I'd thought Namiki was the prettier of the two, but as the afternoon wore on I noticed Fumiko's arching eyebrows and long earlobes. I noticed that the corners of her mouth turned down in a way that made her look pensive. She wasn't beautiful exactly, but I had the sense that what was attractive about her would not, like mere prettiness, fade with time.

Ahead of us, Clifford said something to Namiki, then ducked into a store, leaving her on the sidewalk.

"I'm married," I told Fumiko. "I have a wife."

I wasn't sure how much she understood or why I picked that moment to tell her. I guess I wanted her to know she didn't need to be afraid of me—I desired nothing—but I also wanted to bridge the awkwardness between us by revealing something personal about myself. Fumiko looked up at me and seemed about to smile before turning away to join her friend. I watched them talking for a minute. When Namiki glanced in my direction, Fumiko shot her right hand out to grab Namiki's arm, and I knew they were discussing me. Then Clifford emerged from the store and Fumiko moved to return her right hand to her sleeve, and for an instant her left hand was exposed. I only caught a glimpse, but in that glimpse her skin looked bleached and tight, her fingers curled in upon themselves. In the next instant, her hand vanished and Clifford was calling me over to show me what he had bought, and I couldn't be sure what, if anything, I had seen.

"Look here," he said, brandishing a sword about the length of his forearm. Into its blade was worked a battle scene, tiny men on tiny horses wielding tiny lances, little archers firing minuscule arrows into the air. Except for its size it looked like the samurai swords I'd seen in photographs. "Seppuku," Clifford said, in a growly voice. He pretended to stab himself in the stomach and worked the blade from side to side, hanging his tongue out of his mouth like a cartoon.

I was typing a memo on dental hygiene three days later when Captain Embry emerged from his office and took a seat on the corner of my desk. He was somewhere in his forties, closing fast on chubby. He'd been a policy man before the army, selling life insurance to poor people in Moline, Illinois.

"What'd you do?" he said.

There were fifteen typists in the office. The sound was constant. It was like working in the belly of some rickety machine.

"I don't know, sir."

"I'm serious," he said. "I wanna know whose dick you sucked."

"I haven't sucked anybody's dick, sir."

"Well then, how do you explain the fact that I just got a call inviting you to Bunny's residence?"

My stomach fizzed.

"I don't know, sir."

"I think you sucked somebody's dick." He reached over and pushed my head. Playfully. He seemed proud but mystified. "You old cocksucker. You're to report at 1800. He's showing the Army–Navy game."

Everybody knew Bunny screened movies and newsreels at his residence and that sometimes, as a kind of reward, he invited members of the Honor Guard to join him, but I'd never heard of anyone outside their ranks being included. Captain Embry swore he hadn't done anything to arrange the invitation, said he didn't have the clout to arrange such a thing even if he'd wanted to. He gave me directions and let me off early so I could get a haircut and a shave.

That evening, after a quick supper in the mess, I walked the mile to Bunny's residence. The days were getting longer, and this was the hour when the world looked deep and golden. About halfway, I passed a row of buildings reduced to rubble by our bombs, but even these looked somehow beautiful in the light. A baseball diamond had been set up in the vacant lot across the street. There was no grass but the baselines were chalked and a mound had been built up right where it was supposed to be. I thought of Bunny passing this way every morning on his way to work, every evening on his way home. We all knew his routine. At 0800, he took breakfast with his wife and son, then spent an hour answering his mail. At 1000 hours he boarded his limousine, a coal–black Cadillac liberated from the owner of a sugar plantation in Manila. There were always hundreds of locals hanging around outside the residence hoping for a glimpse of him, hundreds more lining his route. Despite occasional rumors of assassination plots, he refused a protective motorcade. A pair of Honor Guard troops on mo-torcycles led his car through downtown and around Hibiya Park to the Dai Ichi Sogo building. Upon arrival, he put the duty guards through an elaborate manual of arms, more theater than protocol, before disappearing into his office. The Dai Ichi Sogo building had housed an insurance agency before the war and there were plenty of executive offices, but Bunny had chosen a former storage closet for himself, without windows, located in the exact middle of the floor, while his subordinates had views of the park or the Imperial Palace moat. We didn't know what went on in there except through the documents that passed across our desks. Bunny was trying to build a democracy; we knew that much, and to me that sounded fine. At 1300, he returned to the residence for lunch with his wife, followed by a half-hour nap. Then back to the Dai Ichi Sogo building, where he often worked late into the night.

I arrived at the residence fifteen minutes early. I would have killed the time wandering around outside the wall, but there was Clifford standing guard and I didn't want to look like a gawker. When I approached the gate, he winked, then ordered me to halt. He took my name like we'd never met and another guard checked it against a clipboard. A third guard swung the gate open from the inside, and Clifford escorted me up the gravel drive, our boots crunching in time. He didn't say a word and his silence made my heart beat faster. The driveway made a loop in front of the house, and inside the loop a reflecting pool beamed a perfect likeness of the residence back at the sky—ancient white stone, weathered and chipped in places but still regal, like something from a book about medieval times.

At the door, Clifford announced me to yet another guard.

"Private First Class Francis Vancleave."

This new guard rapped on the door and we waited in silence until it swung open from the inside, revealing a Japanese houseboy in a brown kimono. He gestured me inside and I resisted stealing a last look at Clifford before the door closed me into the house. The houseboy led me down a hall and through the kitchen and into a long and narrow room, furnished only with a dozen or so folding chairs and a single cane-bottomed rocker. Red linen curtains were drawn across the windows but there was a gap in one spot and I could see a little boy paddling a little rowboat around a very big swimming pool. The boat had the word *Bataan* painted on the stern. Maybe a dozen officers were sitting around the room, smoking and talking, and I spotted Bunny himself through the haze. Tall, fit for a man his age, hair slicked across his skull. He was wearing bedroom slippers and a tweed coat over his uniform. The houseboy went over and whispered in his ear, and to my surprise Bunny crossed the room to me.

"At ease, Private. We're just here to watch the game."

The room went quiet around us.

"I understand you're a fine typist," Bunny said.

"Thank you, sir."

"That's important. I wish it were not so, but half of soldiering is paperwork anymore."

"Yessir."

"How many words a minute?"

"I'm not sure, sir. Maybe a hundred."

He bugged his eyes, impressed.

"Does that make you the fastest typist in my army?"

"I don't know, sir."

"You ever seen a Japanese typewriter?"

"Yessir."

"Unwieldy. I don't imagine there's a Japanese typist can do better than a hundred words a minute. Not on one of their typewriters. I believe, Private, that makes you the fastest typist in the occupied nation of Japan."

I didn't know how to answer that. I was blushing and sweating. Everybody in the room was watching us.

"You a football fan?" he said.

"Yessir."

"Who's your team?"

"Alabama, sir."

"You don't like Army?"

"I like Army fine, sir."

"But if you had to choose?"

After a moment, I said, "Roll Tide, sir."

He stared down his nose at me for a second then, gradually, let a smile creep over his lips. He turned without another word and took a seat in the rocker. The rest of us scattered among the folding chairs. Bunny stuffed a pipe, lit it with a match, puffed until it was smoking. "All right, Uki," he said, and suddenly the lights went out and the projector was beaming over our heads. Clifford told me afterward that Bunny had had the footage shipped directly from West Point and that he watched the game at least once a week. It had been played back in November, of course, and all of us knew the outcome—Navy won 17–10—but you would have thought Bunny was seeing it for the first time. He cheered wildly when Army did something well and shouted himself hoarse when they did not. Now and then, he launched into monologues on strategy, how Army might have won if they'd had the sense to play as he instructed.

Hours later, after I'd retraced my route in the dark and had a beer to settle my nerves and dozed off imagining how I would relate the events of the evening in a letter to my mother, Clifford came in smelling of liquor and shook me awake.

"Well?" he said.

"Well what? I'm asleep."

"Oh, c'mon," he said. "Wake up, Van. You had a good time, right?"

That's when it dawned on me.

"Are you responsible for tonight?"

He shrugged. "I did somebody a favor. No big deal."

I was used to Clifford being cryptic on certain subjects, so I didn't press. What was of greater interest was why he'd called in this favor for my benefit.

When I asked, he said, "You're my roommate."

"Be serious."

He looked at his hands, looked back up smiling.

"I owed you one," he said.

III

That spring, Emperor Hirohito held his own umbrella in the rain to announce his endorsement of what the locals called "MacArthur's Constitution" and a new National Diet was elected, the first time in history women had voted in Japan, and the International Military Tribunal was gaveled into session, initiating war crimes trials, but none of these things had any real bearing on my life.

Every Tuesday after supper, I played penny-ante poker with a bunch of enlisted men from the OPS, Allen Duckworth and Walter Jernigan and Rudy Grand, among others. Eguchi dealt for tips. The stakes were negligible, but we were grave about our skill at cards. We squinted at our hands and sucked our teeth like there were hundreds in the pot. The most I ever won was two bucks. The most I ever lost was ninety cents.

Some of the men from the barracks organized a sightseeing trip down to Hiroshima one weekend, but I said no thanks. We'd all seen newspaper photos of mushroom clouds and we'd heard the phrase "splitting atoms," but nobody had any idea what that really meant. For some reason, when I thought of the bomb, I imagined a star rising out of nothing, like the flare of a super-powered match, this tiny glimmer expanding, breathing, heating up, turning concrete and steel to dust, until finally the star collapsed, leaving the world cold and black where it had been. That was nothing I wanted to see.

In May, I signed up for a Japanese language class. You didn't really need to speak the lingo to get by—the locals were picking up English in a hurry—but I liked the class, liked the language itself, how far removed every word was from its English counterpart. Rice was *kome* or *gohan* in Japanese, depending on whether it was cooked or not. Bird was *tori*. Love was *koigokoro* or *ai* or *aijou* or *suki* or *ren'ai* or *aikou* or *koi*.

The class was taught by a Staff Sergeant from Honolulu named Phil Takashi. We met every Saturday from 1500 to 1630 and afterwards, I'd do whatever homework we'd been assigned so I wouldn't have to worry about it the following week. Then I'd treat myself to a bowl of noodles at a sake bar I'd found and practice my Japanese on the waitresses. This place was in the Yurakucho district and as I walked, I'd rename the world. Tree. *Ki.* Leaf. *Ha.* Flower. *Hana.* Sidewalk. *Hodou.* Soldier. *Gunjin.* Whore. *Pansaku.* Or panpan in GI parlance. At night, in the Yurakucho district, panpan girls were everywhere. They smoked and teased and sent young boys over with indecent propositions. "Hey Hey GI, you meet my sister." It didn't feel as tawdry as it sounds. The windows were lit with paper lanterns and the girls all smelled like ginger and you knew those boys weren't anybody's brother. They were young enough that if you turned them down, they'd hit you up for bubble gum or chocolate.

I'd arrive just as things were getting started. The bar would be lively with panpan girls wolfing a meal before heading off to work and local men, brushed with soot, half drunk, an hour or two from calling it a night. There were generally a few GIs, but not so many that the place lost its foreign charm. I'd take a stool and study the menu for a while, despite the fact that I couldn't read it—in class, we learned phonetically because Sergeant Takashi said the characters were too difficult for pea brains like us—and I always ordered the same thing: *kitsune udon*. Thick noodles in a salty broth with fried bean curd. Plus a cup of sake. I didn't care for sake really, but I was trying to learn a taste. Like a half-tuned radio station, chatter buzzed around my ears, and I enjoyed the feeling of being able to pluck an occasional word out of the air.

So it went every Saturday for a month until the night I spotted Clifford and Eguchi sitting in the corner with another man, local, his back to me. This other man was talking fast, slapping the table with his palm. Every so often Eguchi interjected, and I figured he was translating. Clifford listened with narrowed eyes. When the man was finished, Clifford smiled the smile he'd given me when I asked him to clean up his toenails. He shook his head, no, then stood and the others stood with him, and I noticed Clifford was wearing a sidearm. As they approached my stool, I waited for him to recognize me but his eyes were faraway.

It was Eguchi who said, "Look here, Major Clifford. It Major Van."

Clifford blinked at me a second.

"I'll be damned." He put his hand on my shoulder and leaned in close and I could tell he was drunk. "What brings you here, Major Van?"

"Nothing. Noodles."

"Hell with that," he said. He turned to Eguchi and the other man. "Fuck off, you two." Eguchi started to leave but the third man stared at Clifford for a moment. I could see now that he was about my age, his features distinguished by con- stellations of moles on both cheeks—a symbol of good luck in Japan—and the wisps of a new mustache. Eguchi took his arm and dragged him between the tables and out the door.

When they were gone, Clifford pointed at my cup of sake on the bar.

"That yours?"

I told him, "Yeah," and he downed what was left.

"You're with me," he said.

He'd parked his jeep around the back. There was a boy, maybe nine or ten years old, sleeping in the driver's seat. Clifford rapped his knuckles on the boy's forehead and the boy came to, rubbing his eyes and grinning like he'd been interrupted in the middle of a pleasant dream. Clifford said, "Go on home now. Go to bed," and pressed a few coins into the boys hand. I figured he'd engaged the boy to keep an eye on the jeep while he was inside. The boy hopped out and wandered off, counting his money, and Clifford took his place behind the wheel. He drove combat-style, with the windshield down. You kept the windshield down so the glass wouldn't catch a glare and make you a better target. Or so I'd been told. Driving like that in peacetime was a way to let everybody know you'd been in the thick of it.

I had to talk loud over the wind.

"Are we going to the Oasis?"

He shook his head. "Namiki's working tonight."

I knew he'd been seeing her without me since the Ginza, but he hadn't shared much in the way of detail. For a second, I couldn't figure why he'd want to stay away, and then it dawned on me that he didn't want to watch her dancing with other men. There were no streetlamps in this part of the city and the buildings blurred past, headlights jerking side to side when Clifford veered around potholes in the street.

"How's Fumiko?" I said.

All of a sudden Clifford looked over and socked me on the arm. The jeep lurched, and I had to grab the wheel to keep us from running up on the curb.

"I knew it!" he shouted.

"What?"

"You want to fuck her."

"No."

"My man Van has had enough of self-abuse."

"Leave me alone," I said.

Inside of an hour, Clifford had gotten me as drunk as I'd ever been, and what I remember of that night I remember in hazy snatches, but I was still sober when he parked the jeep in front of an industrial-looking building in another part of the city I'd never seen. There was a milling, shifting line of Japanese men waiting to be admitted to whatever was inside. They glared when Clifford led me past them and around to a back door. He knocked with the butt of his pistol and the door was answered by a local in a pinstripe suit. Clifford said something in pidgin Japanese—I heard Eguchi's name and the word *tomodachi*. Friend. The man took note of the pistol, turned, and preceded us up three flights of stairs to a table in the back of a vast loft space, like the attic of a warehouse, which is probably exactly what it was. There were a dozen other tables scattered in the shadows. Mismatched chairs staggered in uneven rows away from the tables and toward a stage against the opposite wall. Across the stage was hung a velvet curtain with gold fringe, tattered but beautiful. I remember the luxuriousness of that curtain seemed out of place in such a practical setting. Clifford ordered for both of us, something called *katsutori soku*. I'm not sure what it was but it tasted like fruit and kerosene, and after my first glass the night began its skid into oblivion.

I remember that the room was full and hot and smoky and loud. I remember that ours were the only white faces and I felt both uncomfortable and privileged, as if Clifford were inducting me into some secret club. He was obviously drunk, but he possessed that veteran drinker's gift for leveling off at a plateau, after which he kept pouring *katsutori soku* down his throat without additional perceptible effect. When I asked him what was behind the curtain, he just said, "You'll see."

At one point, later, he leaned across the table and said, "That man was a communist."

"What man?"

"In the sake bar. With me and Eguchi."

"Oh," I said, already too far gone to imagine why he was telling me or what I should say about that or how this information applied to my life, now, in this place, which was beginning to glow and shimmer around the edges like a mirage.

Later still, he said, "Namiki wants me to get her an apartment. I keep telling her I'm a fucking corporal. I'm not made of money. But she won't let me take her to a hotel. She'll only come across if I get her a place of her own."

I remember thinking that Clifford was being played, and then he bolted to his feet and backhanded me across the face, knocking me out of my chair, and I realized that in my stupor I must have said the words aloud. In the next instant, he was kneeling at my side, demanding that somebody bring some goddam ice, though ice was rare as diamonds outside Little America.

Likely I remember that second moment because Clifford's blow rendered me briefly clear-headed, but the first I wouldn't recall until weeks later, when suddenly his words leaped into my mind like someone was twisting my memory into focus with a knob. The rest of our conversation—and there was hours of it— remains lost in fog. Through it all was threaded the show itself, the reason for the stage and that splendid curtain, the reason all those men had come. When the curtain peeled back the first time, a complete hush fell over the crowd, no sound except the squeaking of pulleys. It took a moment to understand what I was seeing. In the middle of the stage was a huge gilt frame, and inside the frame was a kind of high-school-musical rendering of Botticelli's *Venus,* every detail re-created with painted plywood and papier-mâché. Except rising from the clam shell was a very real Japanese woman in a wig. She was naked, like the Venus in the painting, though in this case you could discern the dark triangle of her pubic hair. She held the pose for a minute or two, let us drink her in, then the curtain squeaked shut again, and gradually the men were released from her spell and our voices rose to fill the room until the stage could be reset and the whole business was repeated with another re-creation. I've already stated the case against my memory, and even if I hadn't been so drunk I didn't know enough about art to recognize many of the paintings, but

I remember women under trees and in bathtubs and on rumpled beds, all of them naked and pale, all bathed in the perfect silence of our adoration.

In June, something happened that made headlines in every newspaper in Japan. A local carpenter had been hired to build bookshelves on one of the upper floors of the Dai Ichi Sogo building. One evening, as he was riding the elevator down for the night, it stopped on the fourth floor and Bunny, along with a pair of aides, stepped on. The carpenter tried to bow his way out, intending to let Bunny have the elevator to himself, but Bunny insisted that he remain.

The man was so moved by the experience he wrote a five page letter to the *Asahi* newspaper. He described the incident with boggling thoroughness of detail and offered this commentary:

> I have reflected on the courtesy of General MacArthur for many days, and I realize that no Japanese general or diplomat would have done as he did. I would go so far as to assert that never has a man of such character held sway over Dai Nippon.

The *Asahi* printed the letter in full and by week's end every newspaper in Japan, along with a fair number around the world, had picked up the story. *Life* and *Newsweek* ran short articles and photos of the carpenter—at home and with his tools and in the famous elevator. A writer named Akira Nimura wrote a one-act play called *The General and the Carpenter,* which debuted a month after the incident and ran nightly through the summer and into fall. The locals had long admired Bunny from afar, the way they had admired their own Emperor before the war, but the story humanized him, made his greatness tangible and real. Before the elevator, they would never have presumed to write to him directly—the doors of extraordinary men, they seemed to think, should not be darkened by ordinary concerns —but in the weeks following the elevator incident Bunny received almost five thousand personal letters. A Japanese policeman wrote to request a pair of GI combat boots. A Buddhist priest wrote that he, not Emperor Hirohito, should be living in the Imperial Palace. Mothers wanted child-raising advice, and several women wrote asking him to serve as their stud in order that they might bear great children. Sick people wrote for cures, and prostitutes asked for protection against venereal diseases, and farmers wanted Bunny to temper the floods in the coming rainy season, and the grief-stricken requested safe passage to the next life for their loved ones.

I know all this because Bunny made up his mind that every person who took the time to write him a letter should receive an individual reply, all of which passed through the OPS for typing. For the most part, his responses were little more than form letters. *I am grateful for your note and sympathize with your concern but such requests must be taken up with the proper authorities.* Or *I appreciate your confidence and will hold you in my prayers but requests of this nature must be addressed to an authority far higher than my own.*

Eventually, actual form letters were printed up to serve the purpose but a great deal of that early correspondence was so personal and particular it couldn't be easily dispensed with. For a month, twelve typists, including myself, were diverted to the task, and Bunny was so distracted that the machinery of occupation nearly ground to a halt while he focused on his love affair with the people of Japan.

Captain Embry sent me up to Bunny's office one day with a batch of letters that required a signature before mailing. Usually, letters were left with one of his aides, but that day, Bunny himself was in the outer office when I arrived. He was in the middle of a conversation with his wife. Mrs. Bunny was petite and attractive, dark-haired, wearing a navy blue dress with lace trim at the collar and the sleeves. I thought I could hear traces of a southern accent in her voice.

"I'm not talking about a big production," she was saying. "Just presents and cake and some of the officers' children. A little party at the residence."

There was no aide in sight and I wasn't sure what to do so I stood there holding the letters and trying to draw as little attention to myself as possible. Neither Bunny nor Mrs. Bunny acknowledged my arrival.

"But it'll turn into a big production," he said. "You'll have your party and the next thing I know the Russian ambassador will be in my office with hurt feelings because he wasn't invited."

"It's Arthur's birthday," Mrs. Bunny said. "He's a little boy and he'll be eight years old and you'll just have to deal with the Russian ambassador when the time comes."

I remembered the boy I'd seen paddling a rowboat in the pool behind the residence. Bunny's son. I was holding a box of letters to people who imagined his father had power over all that is seen and unseen.

Mrs. Bunny, however, seemed unimpressed.

"Oh, and I heard about a magician," she said. "Local fella. Breathes fire and swallows swords, all that stuff. For his finale, he turns a cricket into a butterfly."

"Is a magician really necessary?"

"Unless you can turn a cricket into a butterfly, we'll be needing entertainment for the children."

Bunny didn't answer, and Mrs. Bunny adjusted a badge on her husband's chest. "I'll take care of everything," she said. "You just make sure you're present and accounted for."

Then she turned, and they saw me standing there. I tucked the letters under my arm and snapped to attention.

"Hello, soldier," she said.

She kissed her husband on the cheek, wiped away a lipstick print with her thumb, and vanished in a cloud of flowery perfume. Bunny told me to put the letters on the desk.

"I remember you," he said. "The fastest typist in Japan."

I was surprised and flattered.

"You married?" he said.

"Yessir."

"Where you from?"

"Alabama, sir. Mobile."

"Then you know about Southern girls."

"Yessir."

"Lord have mercy," Bunny said.

I waited for him to dismiss me but he did not. He picked up the letters, rifled through them. He pulled one out and laughed softly at what he read.

"This is my reply to a woman who wants me to tell her how to break her daughter of wetting the bed."

He looked at me as if waiting for my opinion on the subject, but I didn't know what he wanted me to say.

"Can you turn a cricket into a butterfly?"

"Nosir."

"That's too bad," he said.

The following day was Saturday, and I woke with the idea in mind that I should get Arthur MacArthur a present for his birthday. I don't know why. Likely, part of me hoped to ingratiate myself with Bunny, but another part, no less real, kept picturing a boy alone in a rowboat in a swimming pool in Japan.

Clifford was sprawled and snoring across the room, still in his uniform. I hadn't heard him come in the night before. I headed for the latrine—crapped, showered, shaved. He was still out cold when I returned. There was a letter on the table by the bed. I'd typed it for him just two days before so he could have it ready, as usual, for the mail on Friday. I doubted the penalty for missing Bunny's deadline was all that grave, but it wasn't like Clifford to let things slide. I thought I'd do him a favor, drop his letter at company HQ on my way to shop for Arthur. To my surprise, there were two letters waiting for me. One from my mother, another from my wife. Somehow letters from both of them at once felt like a bad omen. I wasn't ready to read them yet, so I tucked the envelopes in my back pocket and went out into the street. I passed a road crew hanging new signs—the main thoroughfare had recently been rechristened MacArthur Boulevard—and the Red Cross station, where the walls were pasted over with notes in Japanese from locals still seeking information about soldiers who never made it home or family members gone missing in the confusion of the air raids. On the Ginza, I started with the street vendors because I didn't have much to spend on Arthur's present. Partway down the second block, I came upon a pair of GIs, both negroes, both privates, both lanky and tall, ogling Namiki in her display window. They were debating whether or not she was real, and it's true that with her long neck, her expressionless face in profile to the street, she looked lovely enough that she might have been dreamed up in some mannequin maker's workshop. These GIs were pressed and dressed, and I figured they were on leave from a base out in the provinces.

"See there—she blinked."

"I didn't see nothing."

"Ain't nobody keep that still that long."

"She can if she knows the secrets of the Orient."

The one looked at the other like he couldn't believe what he was hearing. I was standing right behind them. I tried to catch Namiki's eye, but if she saw me, she didn't let on.

"What?"

"Secrets of the Orient."

"I heard what you said. I just don't know what you saying."

That's when I cut in. I couldn't stand it. They were too much.

"She's real," I said.

"You hear that?"

"He don't know nothing. He trying to make a fool of you."

"Just wait," I said.

"You know so much, how bout tell me when this place open up?" He pointed at the sign by the door that led downstairs to the Oasis.

I told him and he said, "Will there be ladies?"

I explained about the tickets and the hostesses and so forth and he said, "Whass our chances?"

I laughed and said, "If you want to get laid, try Ueno Station. That's where you'll find the working girls."

"Aw, man," he said, "Willie Wall don't pay for no pussy," and at that precise moment, Namiki shifted her pose and both GIs jumped and squealed and grabbed each other. Then they started in on how the one or the other was so scared, so dumb, and that bad omen feeling lifted from me like a fog. I left them waiting for her to move again, as if movement rather than stillness was the trick of her profession. A little farther down the sidewalk, I found a vendor selling toy soldiers made from salvaged roofing tin. Hand-painted, snipped into action poses, folded in such a way that they could stand. I bought five samurais for a dollar, and by the time we'd settled up I was ready to take a closer look at my mail. The morning was pleasant, summery—a day that would be hot but wasn't yet. I crossed the street to a café and ordered tea in Japanese, a man in full possession of his life.

> *I hate writing this letter but it'll hurt no matter what and better to get it over with. I'm pregnant. There. Now you know. I've been carrying this secret for months but I'll be showing soon and I can't hide it much longer. You'll want to know about the father but I can only tell you that he is no longer in my life. It is enough that I have been unfaithful, that I am a low, despicable woman, that I made a terrible mistake, that I am alone. I wanted to kill myself but*

I couldn't do it. I wanted to get rid of the baby, but I prayed and prayed and I couldn't do that either. Oh, Van. I'm sorry. I know you don't believe me but it's true. Everything happened so fast with you and me. It hardly seemed real, and the longer you were gone the less real it seemed. None of this is any excuse for what I've done, and I'm sure you'll want to ask for a divorce. I'll accept whatever you decide.

I read the letter three times then hoofed back to the Imperial Finance Ministry intending to compose a reply, but I just sat there, my mind filled up with static. The strange thing was I didn't feel anything. I rolled one sheet out, rolled another in like there was something wrong with the paper. This little bird kept lighting on the windowsill, then darting off when it noticed me at the desk. I stared at the keys. I missed my language class. I was still sitting there, hours later, when Clifford showed up. He leaned into the room from the open door.

"You seen that letter?" he said. "It was right there on the table."

"I mailed it for you," I said.

"Oh," he said. "Thanks." Only then did he come inside. It was like he'd been waiting for an invitation, like I'd offered one. He plopped down on the bed and began powdering his feet.

"You wanna get drunk?" I said.

He said, "I've got plans."

I thought maybe, since I'd done him a favor, he'd invite me to tag along but he did not. The little bird flitted down again, spotted me, fluttered off. Slowly, night was falling over Hibiya Park. I watched a local man sweeping the sidewalk. The little bird came and went. Finally, he stayed gone. By the time darkness settled over the city and the barracks had fallen quiet around me, I had yet to type a single word.

After a while, I remembered the tin soldiers and the letter from my mother. The soldiers were in my breast pocket but I couldn't find the letter anywhere. I hadn't read it in my distraction, and now it dawned on me that I'd left it on the table at the café. I trudged back to the Ginza in the dark but the café was closed, the letter nowhere to be found. On impulse, I ducked into the Oasis. I stood at the bar drinking beer for a long time but couldn't get drunk and they didn't serve anything stronger. A band was playing by the dance floor, local musicians doing popular American songs. The music wasn't bad but it was apparent that the singer didn't understand what he was saying. Likely he'd learned the lyrics phonetically, like we did in class, except he didn't waste time on the meaning of the words. Not only was his accent atrocious but his phrasing was all over the place and he kept emphasizing the wrong parts of the lines. I watched Willie Wall and his friend dancing with one girl after another. They must have spent a fortune. I watched Namiki, too. She was a popular choice among the hostesses. When she danced, she hung her wrists over her partner's shoulders and twitched her hips slowly like a cat.

Eventually, I'd had enough beer that I had to use the head. When I came back out, Willie Wall was asking Namiki to dance but she was ignoring him. I was too faraway to hear what he was saying, but it was easy enough to guess what was going on. Lots of locals were scared of negroes. They didn't have negroes in Japan. He'd say something and she'd gaze over his shoulder and pretend she hadn't heard. He'd say something else. Same response. At first, he looked confused. Maybe he thought something was getting lost in the language barrier, but after a minute he realized that he was being snubbed. You could see the emotion change in his face. He grabbed Namiki's wrist and tried to drag her out to dance, but she snatched her arm away. She wouldn't look at him. His friend tried to get him to settle down but he couldn't now. He was being humiliated and he wouldn't stand for that. None of the other hostesses or employees stepped in. Didn't matter that he was a private. Didn't matter that he was black. He was still a soldier. The white GIs were all hanging back, waiting to see what would happen. It would be funny or it would be ugly. Either way it was bound to be entertaining. That's when I remembered Clifford telling me about the Communist and I walked over and tapped Willie on the shoulder and he whirled in my direction.

"Remember me?" I said.

After a second, a kind of angry glaze fell away from his eyes.

"Mr. Know-It-All," he said.

"Right. Listen. You don't want to mess with this one."

"Don't nobody tell me who I can dance with."

"I'm not telling you you can't. I'm telling you you don't want to. Nothing good is going to happen now."

He stood there for a second, rigid as a billy club, and then he seemed to realize the trouble he was causing, the trouble that might be coming next, and his shoulders sagged and he pinched his mouth into line. Finally, he said, "Fuck it," and went fuming off into the crowd. His friend followed him out. The gawkers went back to their business. The whole room breathed.

"Thank you," Namiki said.

A new song was starting up, and without prompting she stepped into my arms. She was soft and warm, close enough that I could feel her heart beat—frantic at first, slowing little by little as we turned. She smelled like American perfume. It was all I could do to keep from bawling. I told her I didn't have any tickets but she let me have the dance for free.

IV

I met my wife at a Fourth of July dance while I was doing basic at Fort Benning. I see no reason to identify her here. Suffice it to say that both her names are nouns—like Hope or Patience, Baker or Lane. I proposed without telling my parents or asking her father for permission. Who knows why she accepted? The base chaplain performed the ceremony, such as it was. For a honeymoon, we took the train to Savannah. Wandered in and out of shops and made small talk like strangers. It was obvious, even then, that we didn't love each other but we pretended otherwise. Back at the hotel, I asked her to do things neither of us had ever done before, all the things the men in my unit told lies about to pass the time. Afterward, slick with sweat, windows thrown open to the night, she talked bravely of the life we might have together after the war, of meeting my parents, of a little house somewhere, children, and I let her voice wash over me, thinking how much my mother would like her and how my father would be charmed and how I could hardly wait another minute to disappear, listening without listening, like hers was a voice on the radio and I was already far away. My wife had it right in her letter. *The longer you were gone the less real it seemed.* This didn't make her confession any easier to take, but neither was I able to muster indignation for very long. Probably she had imagined pining for a boy under fire, a boy she might never see again, and here she was married to a typist. And I'd hardly been a model husband. I'd quit wearing my wedding ring almost as soon as she was out of sight. I'd stayed faithful, that was true, but I wondered now if that wasn't due as much to gutlessness as decency. I suppose I should have been relieved. My wife's infidelity cleaned the slate for me. But the truth is I wasn't relieved at all. I waffled from humiliation to empathy, from bitterness to concern, never able to settle on how I was supposed to feel.

I didn't see much of Clifford the next few weeks. He'd rented a place for Namiki after all, a room at the back of someone else's house in the Oimachi neighborhood. Not as lavish as Namiki had hoped, he told me, but they had access to a kitchen and a privy, and there was a bathhouse down the street. It was nice enough, apparently, that Namiki held up her end of the bargain. He still came around sometimes to pick up a change of clothes or to drop off a letter for me to type, but most mornings he reported for duty directly from her arms.

His arrangement wasn't particularly unusual. Plenty of locals picked up extra cash renting rooms to soldiers and their girls. Mocking the local mispronunciation, we called these girls *onris* because they devoted themselves to *onri wan* soldier rather than accepting money from anyone willing to pay like panpans. What was unusual about Clifford was that he was a corporal and most of the *onri*s belonged to officers. Enlisted men couldn't generally afford the freight. And I knew Clifford was working hard to pull it off. In his most recent letter, he'd informed his mother that he would be sending less money home for a while because he and his roommate—namely, me—had thrown in together on a motorcycle. That was, of course, a lie. Paying for Namiki's room had left him strapped, even with whatever he brought in on the side.

Without Clifford, the room felt big and empty and quiet. I had tried and failed a dozen times to reply to my wife's letter. Eventually, the sight of the Super Speed began to nag me like a toothache, so I returned it to its cardboard case and stowed it under my bed. But even there I could sense its presence, so I began to spend more time away. I'd head over to the Oasis after chow time or walk the quiet footpaths in Hibiya Park, the stars blurry through the heat, the moon big enough to cast shadows, but most nights I loitered in the rec room, where the air was always riotous with Ping-Pong. In the barracks, the most popular variation of the game was called King Pong. According to the rules, one player kept his paddle and his position at the table until another player managed to beat him to 11 points. Then the victor would take his place as the reigning King Pong until he in turn was beaten and so on. There was one player, a mess cook named Gene McCoy, who was particularly serious about his game. Around the same time I began hiding from my typewriter, Gene began a remarkable three-day run as King Pong. Nightly, challenger after challenger rose up to face him, and nightly he beat them back. Most of the men took pride in the speed and power of their respective games, but Gene was all english and control. He made the ball feint and dance. He didn't overwhelm his opponent with power so much as dink him into clumsy, frustrated submission.

On the final night of Gene's reign, Clifford showed up and took a seat off to the side. I hadn't laid eyes on him for several days, and right away I sensed something was wrong. Honor Guardsmen didn't usually mix with the rest of us. They had their own Ping-Pong table down the row, their own habits and haunts. Plus Clifford looked wound up, jittery, his eyes weary and veined. He watched a couple of games before asking if he might have a turn. The gallery gave way with an air of nervous anticipation. I think half of them hoped that Gene would put the Honor Guardsman in his place and the other half hoped King Pong would finally be toppled from his perch.

Clifford played gamely but Gene beat him 11–6. He waited patiently for another turn and was dispatched again, this time 11–3. The third time he circled back to the table, Gene gave him what we called a skunking. That is, if one player reached 7 points without the other player scoring at all, the game was called. On the final point, Gene sliced a backhand over the net that so wrong-footed Clifford he lost his balance and lurched into the table, scooting it several feet across the floor. He stood there, panting, visibly enraged. It looked like he was going to refuse to give way to the next player, and I worried what might happen if one of us asked him to step aside. I was just rising from my seat, wondering how best to approach him, when he dropped the paddle on the table and left without a word. Gene lost the very next game. He was so shaken up, apparently, by the potential of Clifford's anger that his spin went flat and he was dethroned 11–8 by Rudy Grand. But I missed all that. I went after Clifford instead. I found him in bed with his fists buried in his eye sockets.

"You all right?" I said.

He raised one fist, glanced at me, then covered his eye again.

"Namiki threw me out," he said.

"What? Why?"

"I gave her the clap," he said.

It was as difficult to keep from laughing as it was to restrain myself from asking if he was sure she'd gotten the clap from him. I assumed he knew he was infected—so many GIs picked up one disease or another that people wondered about your character if you *didn't* experience painful urination now and then—but even I understood that it was awfully quick for Namiki to be showing signs.

"I don't know why she's so pissed," he said. "I've got her on penicillin. And it's not my fault anyway. How was I supposed to know the whores in this country are diseased?"

"You tell her that?"

"That's right about when she threw me out."

"What're you gonna do?"

"Nothing. She'll take me back. She has to. Who's gonna want her now she's got the clap?"

"What if she doesn't?"

He shrugged. "Rent's paid through the week. If she doesn't take me back by then, it's *sayonara* love shack. She can go home to her parents. She can live on the streets, for all I care."

In the next instant, he yanked his pillow out from under his head and smothered it over his face and did a muffled bellow.

"Who am I kidding?" he shouted. "Fuck me, Van. I'm in love with a Nip girl with the clap!"

Finally, I couldn't stop myself from laughing. He looked so pitiful. He lowered the pillow to his chest and stared at me from his bed.

In the morning, Clifford returned to his rented room and found it vacated, all Namiki's things removed, the only evidence of his occupancy the seppuku sword he'd bought on their first date hanging forlornly over the futon. He cajoled Eguchi, a day later, into accompanying him to her parents' house. He wanted to be absolutely certain that none of his pleas were mangled in translation and he hoped a relative friendly to his cause might prove useful, but even Eguchi was barred admittance by her mother. Convinced, now, that an elliptical approach was best, he tried Fumiko but she not only refused to hear his case, she sent him home with a shiner. As soon as he was in range, even before he'd had a chance to tell her why he'd come, she launched a potato at his head with her good hand.

Finally, he turned to me. His plan was simple: I'd go down to the Oasis, ask Namiki to dance, and convince her to forgive him before the song was through. She couldn't turn me away, he said, because I'd rescued her from the dangerous negro Willie Wall. I had my doubts about his chances, but I agreed to try. Not too many months before, Clifford had expressed his envy of my marriage, and suddenly I found myself jealous of him, jealous even of his heartache. At least he knew what he wanted.

On the evening in question, Clifford double-checked my uniform like he was sending me out on a first date, smoothed a hand along my cheek to check my shave. We rehearsed the script: He loved her, he was sorry, he was in bad shape without her, and he'd do anything to get her back. All of which proved beside the point. Namiki sized me up in the time it took to cross the dance floor. I was just getting started on my spiel when she whispered "OK" into my ear, and I understood that she had been expecting me, that she had made her decision long before I arrived. Probably she had known she would be going back to Clifford even as she packed her things and bolted for her mother's house. Before that moment, I'd been a little bit afraid of her—she was beautiful and, like all beautiful women, inspired a degree of awe. But now, as we danced, I just felt rotten. For suspecting her motives. For doubting her virtue. It didn't matter if I was right. She was out of options. But she was a woman and she was proud, and dignity required her to make a show of what power she had left.

Because the Oasis was situated in a basement, the air was perpetually humid. There were no windows and only two doors, the entrance on the Ginza and a second door that led to an alley behind the building. Both were open now, but the cross breeze died halfway into the room. When Namiki twitched her hips, I could feel actual heat rising from beneath her dress, quick warm puffs, like breath. Her left hand was draped over my shoulder. In her right hand, she held a paper fan printed with Japanese characters and she waved it listlessly but cease-lessly, out of time to the music and without hope of relief.

By the end of the week, before the lease was up, they were back in Oimachi and I was alone again in the barracks and still I hadn't replied to my wife's letter. It wasn't that I didn't want to. It was that the idea of a reply had assumed such proportions in my imagination it was impossible to write.

Then, one afternoon, I received a thank-you note from Arthur MacArthur. My name and rank were printed neatly on the envelope. The note itself was penned in boyish cursive.

Thank you for the tin soldiers you sent for my birthday.
I have an extensive collection of military toys and the
samurais make a fine addition. Last night, they defended
the gates of a forgotten mountain kingdom against a fron-
tal assault by U.S. Marines. They fought valiantly but
were defeated due to lack of firepower. Maybe you would
like to join me one day to play with my extensive collec-
tion of military toys. Thanks again. Most of my other
presents were clothes.

The diction was a shade sophisticated for an eight-year-old, and I couldn't help picturing Bunny perusing early drafts and returning them with corrections. Arthur would be stretched out on the floor writing my note while his father smoked a pipe and read *The Sporting News*. There are few enough ways in life for a boy and his father to get along, but that doesn't mean the father ever stops trying to teach his son to be a man. I imagined Bunny wanted to raise not just a man but a gentleman.

After work, I retrieved the Super Speed from under the bed, dusted it off, returned it to its place on the desk, and dashed off a letter to my wife. *Dashed* is the right word. I was afraid that if I let myself think too much about what I was writing, I'd lose my nerve. I told her I understood—what happened between us had seemed like part of what was happening in the world. I wished her happiness, her and the baby. When it was finished, I stuffed the letter in an envelope and rushed it down to HQ in the dark so I wouldn't have a chance to change my mind.

V

The International Military Tribunal didn't start making headlines until summer was coming to a close. That business up in Nuremberg was getting all the press. Even so, Bunny issued regular statements on the subject and we typed his dispatches, not without a certain morbid curiosity. The names of the defendants were recognizable even to enlisted men: Shimada, Nagano, Tojo. Especially Tojo. Plenty of military criminals had already been tried and executed in the Philippines. Most of us presumed this lot would be hanged as well.

Because he wanted to expose the locals to the impartiality of Western justice and to make them fully aware of the atrocities perpetrated by their former leaders, Bunny opened the trials to the public. Each morning, free passes were issued for half a day's session, but industrious hustlers like Eguchi would spend the night waiting in line, grab up the passes first thing and sell them for top dollar like ticket scalpers back home. Still, the gallery was always full: farmers, students, merchants. People poured into Tokyo from all over to see humbled the men who had set in motion their national humiliation.

Then, in September, a *Newsweek* reporter stationed in Tokyo wrote an article questioning the decision to exempt

Emperor Hirohito from prosecution. This reporter contended that the Emperor had made numerous public statements extolling the righteousness of conquest when the war was going well and exhorting his subjects to fight to the very last man when the tide had turned. Only after we'd dropped the bomb did he change his tune. How could he not be tried? What Bunny did was have the reporter ejected from Japan. He issued a rebuttal, arguing that the Emperor's power had been nominal at best, that he was a puppet of the military and the merchant class. The Emperor was sacred to the Japanese, Bunny said, and good relations would be decimated if he was dishonored. The story that made news, however, at least back in the States, was that Bunny was putting a lid on freedom of the press.

A week later, there was a riot outside the Imperial Palace Gates. I saw the whole thing from a window in the office. Reports varied, but most newspapers agreed that around a thousand young men, perhaps inspired by the controversy, marched into Hibiya Park, everybody chanting and waving red communist flags. Lots of repatriated soldiers in the crowd. Still in uniform. Likely the only clothes they owned. Hard to tell who they were protesting, the army that had beaten them in the field or the Emperor they believed had sent them into battle in the first place. The march itself wasn't the problem. The trouble came when a group of protesters got carried away and tried to cross the bridge, intending—or so it was reported—to drag the

Emperor out of the palace and haul him over to the trials. A nervous policeman, a local, fired into the crowd, then a second, then a third, killing two men, wounding three more. Another dozen were injured in the stampede back across the moat.

It's difficult to describe how it felt when I heard the shots. They sounded flat, like a hand slapping the water, and it took a moment before I even realized what I'd heard. Rudy Grand was watching over my shoulder. He said, "Jesus Christ," and I said, "What?" and then I understood. The crowd surged against itself, half of them still trying to rush the palace and the other half in full retreat.

What most papers failed to report was that, the day after the riot, ten thousand women descended on Hibiya Park at dawn. Without making a single speech, without a word, really, no sound but the shuffling of their feet, they lined up along the length of the moat and knelt in the grass and stayed there until nightfall, a human barrier against those who would harm the Emperor. According to Bunny, the press wasn't interested in silence. They wanted fireworks or nothing at all.

I was shaving one morning while Eguchi mopped around the johns and I decided to ask him what he thought about the trials. Talking to Eguchi was a bit like talking to a newsie in a mob film. There was something touching and comic in the way he blended actual youth with a veneer of premature manhood.

He smoked like a fiend and he could drink more than most GIs and he possessed a remarkable vocabulary of American slang, particularly the bluer elements of the idiom. But he was also still very much a boy. He saluted everybody in the barracks and he begged combat stories from the men who'd seen real action. When he dealt for the Tuesday Night Poker Game, he did not sit so much as perch in his chair, elbows on his knees, bouncing lightly on the balls of his feet and squinting through the haze of smoke from a cigarette clenched between his teeth, while he flicked cards around the table. The men in the barracks delighted in asking his opinion on everything from world events to women trouble. If he recognized the irony in our treatment of him, he played to our expectations like a Hollywood savant. It's also true that Eguchi was thoroughly patched into life in Tokyo, its real and beating heart rather than the surface shine of Little America, and though none of us would have admitted it, I believe we all secretly valued his opinion.

My face was about half shaved when I asked the question, and I watched his reflection as he stopped what he was doing and leaned his weight on the mop.

"You want pass?" he said. "I get pass. Special deal. Five thousand yen."

"I'm just interested," I said.

He looked at me for a moment, then shrugged and started mopping again. "Tell you what. You forget Pearl Harbor, we forget Hiroshima. Fuckin A."

I waited, razor poised, for him to wink or laugh, to reveal that he was just pulling my leg. It is worth noting that often soldiers like myself, who manage to avoid combat and so are never made cynical or disillusioned by the reality of battle, are the ones who take the army most seriously, with the most pride and patriotism. I dragged the razor slowly down my cheek, rinsed it in the basin, brought it up again. Eguchi must have sensed something in my silence. He turned back to the mirror and arranged his features into a smile.

"You sure you no want pass?" he said. "For you, four thousand yen."

All of the above might sound exciting by comparison to my routine, but it would be misleading to suggest that life in Tokyo changed much as summer bled into the fall. After the riot, there passed a day or two of respectful tiptoeing, but inside of a week the city returned to the business of rising from the ashes. Not surprising, I suppose, in a place so done in by war. A few dead communists were hardly worth the effort it took to dig their graves. The debate trickled on in the stateside papers but nobody was paying much attention, and the vast majority of typing that crossed my desk was of a bureaucratic nature too dull to mention here.

I was working on just such an assignment when Bunny himself marched in one day unannounced, trailing a pair of

Honor Guardsmen. We were all so focused on our work that nobody noticed him at first. One of the Honor Guardsmen barked, "Ten—*hut!*" and we scrambled to attention, but somehow Rudy Grand failed to realize what was happening. His desk was at the back of the room, and he couldn't see Bunny because the rest of us were on our feet.

"What the fuck?" he said.

"Watch your mouth, soldier."

At the sound of Bunny's voice, Rudy leaped so abruptly from his chair that he banged his knee on his desk, tipping a cup of coffee onto a stack of papers. He moved to rescue the papers then remembered that Bunny himself was in the office. He didn't know what to do. You could see ripples of indecision playing out across his face.

Bunny sighed. "Go ahead. Clean it up."

Rudy pinched the ruined papers between his thumb and index finger, shook coffee onto the floor, set the papers in the seat of his chair. He stared, perplexed, at the puddle on his desk. After a moment, Bunny fished a handkerchief from his pocket and offered it to Rudy. Rudy accepted, made a few nervous swipes at the spill, tried to return the handkerchief to Bunny.

"Keep it," Bunny said. "Where's your CO?"

"Lunch, sir."

"Fine," Bunny said. "Private Vancleave, remain at your desk. Everybody else get out. I need the room."

The room emptied in a instant. Even Bunny's escort took up a post outside the door. Bunny moved to the open window and gazed down upon Hibiya Park.

"Did you receive a thank-you note from my son?" he said.

"Yessir."

"And in that note did my son not invite you over to play with his extensive collection of military toys?"

"Yessir."

He took a deep breath, squared his shoulders, and clasped his hands behind his back. His posture made me nervous, made the moment feel grave. He addressed himself to the park.

"I'm in a pickle, Private. I've hauled my family, who I love, all the way over to Japan, and it looks like we're going to be here for a while. I want my son to have a normal life— as normal as possible under the circumstances. Currently, there are eleven officers in my command with families in Tokyo, but there's a pecking order and it's important, silly as that may sound. The British Ambassador has a boy about Arthur's age and that would probably be all right, but Arthur's tutor is English and my son is starting to pick up a British accent. He spends most of his time playing with the houseboys, and they always let him win and I have no intention of raising a jack-ass. You follow me?"

"Nosir."

"What I'm asking is for you to come out to the residence and play with my son." When I didn't answer right away, he showed me his profile, that long aquiline nose. "You have a question, Private? You're wondering if this is an order?"

"Not exactly, sir."

"What then?"

"I'm wondering why me, sir?"

"You're white. You're American. You're an enlisted man, so it won't look like I'm playing favorites. My wife is from Tennessee. If my boy is going to have an accent, I'd rather it be a southern drawl than a prissy British lilt. More importantly, you got him a birthday present. You got *him* a present. One he liked. Not something you thought I might like."

Again, I didn't answer.

"Spit it out," he said.

"Does Arthur want me to come, sir?"

"He said so in his note, didn't he?"

"Yessir."

"There you have it."

"Yessir."

"Then you're amenable?"

"Yessir."

"Good. Report to the residence on Saturday at 0900. We'll see how it goes. You will tell no one about our arrangement. Arthur is to believe you are present at his invitation. Understood?"

"Yessir."

He exhaled, then, and the stiffness went out of him.

"You can see the moat from here," he said.

"Yessir."

"You ever read the Emperor's poems?"

"Nosir."

"The Pine is brave/that changes not its color/bearing the snow." Bunny tipped his head back while he recited, and now he let his chin fall to his chest. "Funny little guy. Zero charisma. I'm here to tell you the man is about as charming as a glass of water. Truth is, I intended to use him more sternly but he's like a forty-year-old child. There's an innocence about him. Until we arrived, he hardly ever left the palace. And most of the Japanese had never laid eyes on him. They believe—or they did til we showed up—that the Emperor is a direct descendant of the gods. What interests me is how they've adapted, how they make due. Except for the Reds, these people have got the spirit of the Sermon on the Mount."

I had no idea what he was talking about, but to my great relief he didn't require a reply. Before I could say a word, he rapped his knuckles on the windowsill, bringing our meeting to a close. He about-faced and I saluted and he was gone. For about ten seconds, I was alone. I'd never heard the office so quiet. I walked over to my desk and started typing. I didn't want to be standing there like an idiot when the rest of the men returned.

* * *

I spent the remainder of afternoon fending off questions about what he'd wanted. I said he needed some last minute corrections on a report. I could tell no one believed me, but the flimsiness of my excuse, the secrecy behind it, had the effect raising my stock. I was wise to information beyond their ken.

Just before quitting time, Captain Embry called me in. He was sitting at his desk with his feet propped up, a plug of tobacco in his cheek.

"Close the door," he said.

I did and he said, "All right now. Enough bullshit."

"I'm not sure what you mean, sir."

"Knock it off, Vancleave. I'm not gonna tell nobody."

I started to repeat my explanation, then realized that the more I repeated it the less anybody believed me and the more I sounded like a jerk. I decided to go with a portion of the truth.

"I'm sorry, sir. Bunny ordered me not to tell."

He sized me up with a squint. He spit into a coffee cup. "You old cocksucker," he said.

By the end of the day, this new explanation had made the rounds. Captain Embry told somebody else and that person leaked it around the barracks. I could feel people staring in the mess hall. The truth, the full extent of it, was bound to come out before long and I'd be in for no end of ribbing when it did, but in the meantime "Bunny's orders" seemed to do the trick. At least people stopped asking questions.

*   *   *

It was under these circumstances that I started out for Bunny's residence a second time. The morning was all dew on the grass and birdsong in the trees. Mosquitoes. As I was passing the baseball diamond, it dawned on me that this day marked the anniversary of my arrival in Japan. The occasion called for something, but I didn't know what. At the residence, the guards—none of them Clifford—put me through the same rigmarole as before and the same houseboy led me inside and down the hall to Arthur's room and rapped softly on the door. After a moment, I heard Arthur say, "What do you want?" The houseboy told him his guest had arrived and my face went hot. Twelve months in Tokyo and here I was.

Arthur MacArthur had his father's nose and what I would come to recognize as his mother's sharply tapered eyes. On his father, that nose looked distinguished and on his mother, those eyes looked mirthful and mischievous. On Arthur, the two combined to make him appear petulant and mean.

He hadn't exaggerated about his collection. The walls of his room were lined with display cases all filled up with cast-iron soldiers. He had Spartans and Roman Legionnaires, Persians and Carthaginians for them to fight. He had crusading knights and infidel Moors. He had Minutemen and Hessians and Redcoats. He had Wellington's dragoons and Jeb Stuart's cavalry and doughboys from Belleau Wood. The soldiers were so beautifully painted that many of the generals were recognizable: George Washington and Napoleon and Robert E. Lee.

I was half surprised not to find his father on the shelf. In addition to the troops, he had a wide array of engines of war, catapults and siege towers, howitzers and Sopwith Camels and Sherman tanks. He had submarines and Viking ships. He had gunboats from the Spanish Armada. The tin samurais I'd given him were shabby-looking next to the rest, but Arthur didn't distinguish according to quality. He'd situated the samurais on the shelf in their proper place in history, and I was pleased to find them there.

What Arthur liked to do was pit a general from one historical period against a general from another. Napoleon against Hannibal, for example, or Robert E. Lee versus Julius Caesar. The rules of the game became clear in a hurry. No matter whom he was commanding, Arthur triumphed because of superior strategy and daring in the field. I remembered what his father said about letting him win, but it was too much trouble to raise a stink. The actual battles didn't take long. It was the setting up that filled our time. The troops had to be arranged just so before Arthur was ready to begin.

"You can't do that," he said, when I had established my legionnaires in what I thought was a strong position to ambush his Confederate cavalry. "The Romans always advance in a phalanx."

"You know a lot about this stuff," I said. "Your dad must be real proud."

Arthur was lining up his rebels, Jeb Stuart out front, saber up, ready to lead the charge. They would be supported by a battery of Napoleonic artillery on the high ground of his bed. Likely, the barrage would wipe out most of my legionnaires before Jeb Stuart crossed the field. Then he'd send the samurais in behind the cavalry to mop up what was left of my front line and all I had in reserve were a handful of Sam Houston's volunteers.

"Is your father a soldier?" he said.

I said, "He's a tugboat captain," and Arthur looked interested. I knew how he felt. The open sky and all that. Dicey currents and hidden shoals. A world composed almost entirely of men. Arthur asked me to tell him more so I described the way the tugs pushed barges around in the lacework of rivers in the south.

"He was gone a lot," I said. "Two or three weeks at a time."

"He didn't take you with him?"

"He couldn't. That was against the rules."

"If he's the captain, can't he make his own rules?"

"It's not his boat. He works for the men who own it."

I thought he might be disappointed, but he said, "My father is gone a lot, too. He works for the President. He takes us with him to his posts when he can, but sometimes it's too dangerous."

"Do you like it here?"

Arthur shrugged. "I haven't earned enough points yet to go home."

The army used a point system, based on time in service and the nature of an assignment and individual records and so on, for determining when a soldier would be discharged, and I imagined Bunny explaining this to his son, telling him that he could expect no less from his family than he expected of his troops.

"At least you're with your dad. I'm sure you miss him when he's gone."

"Did you miss your dad?" he said.

I nodded but said, "My mother and I did all right. It was my mother taught me how to type. I only let her give me lessons on the nights when my father was away."

"Why?"

"I was embarrassed, I guess. I thought typing was for girls. I didn't think my dad would like it."

"Did he?"

"I don't know."

Arthur frowned at his line of horsemen.

"Let's be allies instead," he said. "You be Robert E. Lee and I'll be Hannibal."

"We'll be unstoppable," I said.

After many victories, the houseboy returned and told Arthur it was time for lunch. I followed him toward the kitchen. Bunny's voice met us in the hall. "I'm not about to let that idiot back in the country. I don't care what the papers say. I won't be bullied. No reporter is going to undermine the progress we've made over here."

Mrs. Bunny said, "It'll be all right, General. The people love you. You know that. The press will come around."

"Meanwhile, I'm supposed to tolerate half-wit editorialists? I haven't the patience."

They went quiet when we came in. Mrs. Bunny set Arthur's plate on the table and smiled at me. Bunny was smoking his pipe and reading the *Times*.

"You boys have fun?" he said.

"Yes, sir." Arthur slid into his chair. "Can Van come back next week?"

Bunny peeked at me over the page.

"All right," I said, and he nodded, once, sealing the deal.

VI

....

It didn't take long for word to spread. I raised a dollar at the Tuesday Night Poker Game and Rudy Grand said, "Damn, Van, your pockets must be full of babysitting money," and the rest of the men picked up the joke—Did I have to change his diapers? Did Arthur make me cut the crusts off his sandwiches? If I'd let myself make fun of Arthur or Bunny or any of it, I could have turned the joke around, gotten us all in on it together, but something stopped me, and over the next few weeks, as my Saturdays with Arthur became a regular engagement, I was glad. The ribbing didn't let up exactly, but I began to hear a hint of envy in it and my embarrassment faded with repetition and the truth is, I looked forward to those mornings after a while. If it was raining, we plotted great campaigns and fought desperate battles in his room, but if the weather was nice we'd toss a football in the yard or something, feeling a pleasant kind of pressure to enjoy the outdoors before the season changed again. Arthur wasn't much of a ballplayer, but he was game and I knew he wanted to impress me, which made me like him more. I should say that, like Arthur, I'm an only child. I had no younger siblings to look up to me when I was a kid, and that's probably one reason I took such pleasure in his admiration.

This is not to mention that he was Bunny's son. My father made a better-than-average wage, likely more than you'd expect, enough that we could afford a little house with a big front porch in a decent neighborhood—lots of old oaks and azaleas and Spanish moss, a dentist on our right, a middle-school vice principal on our left, the manager of a hardware store across the street. It was a decent life, better than most of the men I'd met in the army, but it was nothing like Arthur's existence at the residence. The MacArthurs had four dogs: Blackie, a cocker spaniel; Brownie, a terrier; Koko, a Brittany spaniel; and the puppy, Taro, a white Akita named after Arthur's favorite houseboy. All four dogs tagged along if we played outside, and when they barked and scrambled off toward the house, I knew they heard Bunny's Cadillac on the gravel returning him for lunch.

One Saturday, on the way out to the residence, I noticed that *Anchors Aweigh* was playing at the theater downtown. Gene Kelly, Frank Sinatra. It had been a big hit in the States the year before, had finally made it overseas. I thought maybe Arthur would be interested and asked his parents for permission to take him to a matinee. Bunny deferred to Mrs. Bunny. She was reluctant, but Arthur was so excited by the prospect that she agreed.

Because of the matinee I arrived later than usual the following week—Bunny had already come home for lunch and gone again—and a houseboy led me to her room, a kind of parlor with a sitting area and a writing desk. Lots of knickknacks, jeweled cigarette cases, lacquered fans. A window looked out over an alley of maples behind the house, branches heavy with misting rain. She told me to have a seat and I waited while she finished jotting something down.

"Are you thirsty?" she said.

"No ma'am."

She came around the desk and took the chair across from mine.

"I'll get right to business then," she said. "I'm not sure this little excursion of yours is such a good idea." She pinched her lips into a smile. "Please remove your hat," she said, and I did, a prickle of shame crawling like an insect along my spine. I wasn't sure if the shame was born of the fact that I'd forgotten to remove my hat or because Mrs. Bunny had ordered me to do so or because I'd been so quick to comply. Mrs. Bunny went on. "That's better. I'll be honest, Private; I was against this arrangement from the beginning. You and Arthur, I mean. It's nothing personal. You seem a decent sort. But the General had his reasons so I went along. Arthur has become attached to you and he'd never forgive me if I went back on my promise to let you take him to the movies. I just want us to be clear before you go. The driver will carry you to the theater, drop you off, wait for you outside, and bring you directly home. There will be no stops in between. While you are out of this house, Arthur is your responsibility. If you return him to me with a hair out of place, I'll see to it that you're court-martialed by morning. Perhaps you think that such a thing is beyond my power, but I assure you I am entirely capable of keeping my word. Do we understand each other?"

"Yes ma'am."

Mrs. Bunny crossed her legs, draped her wrists over one knee. In an instant, without a perceptible change in her facial expression, her demeanor somehow went from ominous to sociable.

"My husband tells me you're from Mobile," she said.

"Yes ma'am."

"Do you know the Blackfords by any chance?"

"I don't think so, ma'am."

"What about the Harringtons, Lola and Jimmy? Surely that name rings a bell."

"You mean the congressman?"

"I went to school with Lola. We spent a lovely weekend at their place on Point Clear just before the war."

I heard Arthur's footsteps on the stairs and he came tearing into the room ahead of an apologetic-looking houseboy, and Mrs. Bunny morphed again before my eyes, this time from socialite to mother. She made Arthur give her a hug and walked us to the door, where we were met by the driver, a negro named Ridges, who escorted Arthur to the car under an umbrella. When I climbed into the passenger seat, without looking at me, he said, "You in back," and Arthur laughed, and I slid onto the leather seat at his side, embarrassed again and irritated with him, rather than Ridges, for reasons I couldn't have explained.

The car, a navy blue Packard, was not as impressive as Bunny's Cadillac, but it was waxed and polished and raindrops pearled and glistened on the chrome, still a sight, I thought, to the locals. There would be no doubt that somebody important was inside. And the scene, as we rounded the curve along the baseball diamond, was almost comical. A dozen or so boys not much older than Arthur were in the middle of a game—it wasn't raining hard enough to keep anybody inside—and the ball had just been popped up as we came into view, an easy out, but the boys were so entranced by our passage that it dropped between second base and center field, bounced twice, and trickled slowly over the grass, the only thing moving in the tableau of their wonder.

"We should come down here sometime," I said. "Maybe they'll let us play."

"I doubt my mom would go for that," he said, and I figured he was right. I also thought I heard an edge of worry in his voice. He didn't have much experience with ordinary kids. Irritation again—at his anxiety, his pamperedness. But I didn't want to be irritated. To change the subject, I asked his favorite movie star and he said, "John Wayne," without hesitation.

"What about Gary Cooper?" I said. "You ever see *The Plainsman*?"

Arthur nodded. "Pop showed it at the house. It's pretty good, but *Stagecoach* is better."

He was spoiled, yes, but he was so marooned by the nature of his life, he was ignorant of his privilege. It's possible he was the loneliest person I'd ever met. He knew only isolation, and this made him immature in certain ways. He'd lived all over the world, had every material advantage, but as we neared the theater, in his excitement, he reached across the seat and took my hand in the manner of a child much younger than himself and all my irritation ebbed away. Ridges left the car running and came around to Arthur's door and walked him to the marquee under the umbrella, then handed me the umbrella so I could walk him back.

The theater was about three quarters full, more locals than GIs, and *Anchors Aweigh* pretty much what you'd expect—two sailors on liberty, lots of singing and dancing, plenty of romance. I worried that Arthur wouldn't like it, but whenever I glanced over I could see his eyes shining in the light from the projector, his face pleasantly empty and relaxed, a fistful of popcorn rising toward his mouth. Afterward, as we filed up the long aisle toward the lobby, I asked him what he thought, and he said, "It was great."

"Really? You liked it?"

"The part where Gene Kelly danced with the cartoon mouse—I thought that was pretty neat."

"Yeah," I said. "It was."

The first thing I noticed in the lobby was a crowd of locals bunched up against the windows, everybody chattering in hushed, excited Japanese.

"What's going on?" Arthur said.

"I don't know."

I took hold of Arthur's wrist, waded in. I couldn't see anything but more people outside and the Packard at the curb. To my surprise, I spotted Namiki in the throng, craning on tiptoe like all the rest. I reached over an elderly man to tap her shoulder and she looked at me blankly, lost in whatever was happening, unable to place me in the moment, then recognition passed over her face. The crowd was thick enough that it swelled in behind us as we moved closer together, and we had no choice but to give way.

"It is said that General MacArthur's son is here." Her eyes were bright with expectation, her English hesitant but much improved since I'd seen her last. That's when she noticed Arthur. She looked at him, then back at me, confused, surprised, impressed, then at Arthur again, and I felt washed with unexpected pride. She blushed and started a bow but I put a hand on her arm, pressed a finger to my lips. I winked at Arthur.

"Let's have a little fun," I said.

Keeping a grip on Arthur's wrist, I circled around behind the knot of people at the window and shouted, "All right. Clear the way. VIP coming through," and there was a perceptible intake of breath from the crowd, a new tenor to their murmuring, and like magic they policed themselves backward to form an aisle from the lobby through the door and out across the sidewalk to the car, bowing as we passed, me leading the way, then Arthur, then Namiki, beaming, thrilled, swept along behind us as if caught up in our wake. Ridges saw us coming and hustled around to open the door. Even overcast, the day was too bright after the darkness of the theater and the rain brushed my face like walking through a spiderweb and somehow Namiki tumbled into the car behind us before Ridges could cut her off. I realized just as we were all pouring into the backseat that I'd forgotten the umbrella. I could see it clearly, propped against an empty seat, dripping a puddle on the floor. Then someone in the crowd shouted, "God bless USA!" and someone else shouted, "MacArthur live long time!" The door slammed shut behind us and the crowd closed in around the car and as Ridges jostled his way back to the driver's side and fell in behind the wheel, we were washed in good wishes and cheers.

"Who the fuck is that?" he said, meaning Namiki.

He yanked the gearshift, nudged us out of the crowd. I said, "Watch your mouth."

Our eyes met in the rearview mirror. He shifted his gaze to Arthur and Namiki, weighing, I thought, the repercussions of cursing in front of Bunny's son against responsibility for this woman in the car. "The missus ain't gone like it," he said, and only then did I pause to examine my motives. "Not one bit," he said, and it dawned on me that I'd been showing off, inspired by Namiki's admiration. She was wearing sandals and a belted white dress—gifts from Clifford, I presumed, straight from the PX—and she was lovely in her American clothes and she knew me only as the roommate, a stand-in, a messenger, someone to occupy her friend. I sensed something else as well, something petty behind my desire to impress Namiki, a need to rebel that had been building in me since my meeting with Mrs. Bunny. The elation I'd felt as we paraded through the crowd evaporated, leaving me limp.

"I forgot the umbrella," I said.

Ridges flicked his eyes at me again, this time with more confidence. On either side of me, Arthur and Namiki were twisted in their seats, watching the crowd disappear behind us as we pulled onto MacArthur Boulevard. We drove in silence for a minute, Arthur and Namiki exchanging smiles across the seat, both of them shy, intimidated by the other. At the next intersection, Ridges eased over to the curb.

"All right, miss," he said to Namiki. "That's far enough."

I wanted to argue, insist that he at least take her to the nearest bus stop, but there was no point in it and all the steam was gone from me. He was right. Mrs. Bunny would be furious that I'd let Namiki into the car at all. It wasn't just that she was a stranger, a woman, a local. She was a dance hall girl, some enlisted man's *onri wan*. In Mrs. Bunny's eyes, that would make her little better than a whore. To my surprise, Arthur stepped in. "But it's raining. We can't leave her here." He turned to Namiki. "Where are you going?"

Namiki dropped her eyes. "Ginza," she said. "Work."

"Take her there," Arthur said.

"I don't think that's a good idea, Mister Arthur. Your momma say—"

"Take her," Arthur said.

Ridges hesitated and I felt two things: On the one hand I was vaguely proud of Arthur for standing up for her, for seizing the initiative, but on the other I felt sorry for Ridges all of a sudden. No matter what happened now, he couldn't win. Though it was my fault, he would be saddled with a measure of the blame for Namiki's presence. If he did what Arthur said, his liability would be compounded by making us late, keeping Mrs. Bunny waiting. If he refused, he would be delivering home a spoiled, sulky child made unhappy by his decision, and who knew what effect that might have on his life down the road.

"Listen, Arthur," I said. "If we take her, you can't tell your mom. You understand? Your mom'll have all our hides. We'll tell her we got caught in traffic or something."

Arthur nodded, titillated, I thought, by the idea of our deception, and I wondered how much of all this Namiki understood. Again, I met Ridges's eyes in the mirror but I could no longer read his face. Arthur extended his hand to Namiki across my legs. "I'm Arthur," he said. "My dad is the Supreme

Commander of Allied Forces in the Pacific." I nearly laughed out loud. He'd used Bunny's official title, but you hardly ever heard it like that—everybody just used the acronym, SCAP—and it sounded oddly formal, almost royal. Namiki took his hand in both of hers and bowed three times in quick succession, making a noise in the back of her throat each time—*hai, hai, hai*—like she'd been arrested by a sneezing fit.

"This is Namiki," I said, and Arthur said, "Pleased to meet you, Miss Namiki," and we rolled on through Little America, turning heads as we passed.

Bunny's Cadillac was parked out front when we returned. I wanted to make a quick getaway but I knew that would look suspicious, so I followed Arthur inside and we found his mother in the kitchen, peering over the shoulder of her cook, supervising dinner preparations the way her husband managed battle plans. Arthur was still buoyant from the afternoon, running on excitedly about the movie and what a good time he'd had, not a word about Namiki. After a few minutes, Mrs. Bunny dismissed me and I told Arthur I'd see him next week, relief flooding through me like we'd pulled off a crime.

On my way out, Bunny called to me from down the hall. He was reclined on a sofa in a sitting room, feet on the floor, head and shoulders propped on a nest of pillows, an unlit pipe jutting from the corner of his mouth like a sarcastic remark.

He was scratching notes on a yellow legal pad. All around him, the floor was littered with files.

"Nice day?" he said.

"Yessir."

"Good movie?"

"Yessir."

"Listen," he said, and I worried for a moment that the tentacles of his influence ran so deep he'd already heard about Namiki, but all he said was, "What's Alabama gonna do this season? I saw in the paper where they lost to Tulane. That's quite an upset."

"They'll be all right, sir. They've got Harry Gilmer."

He drummed his pencil on the pad. "Let me ask you something. What's your opinion of morale in my command? Seems to me morale has fallen off a little since the summer."

As far as I knew, morale was fine and I wondered if his concern didn't stem from the way the press had been treating him, if the morale in question might be his own. But I wasn't about to tell him that.

"No matter," he said. "I've got an idea that just might help right the ship."

"Is that so, sir?"

"Were you aware that Bill Bertelli is attached to the Second Marines?"

"Bullet Bill, sir? The fullback?"

"Not just any fullback. He was a two-time All-American at Holy Cross."

"He's here in Japan, sir?"

"He is indeed. And not just him. Calvin Thomas is a coreman at the field hospital in Yokohama, and Marty Vaughn is a cook on the *Bonhomme Richard,* just off the coast."

I knew the names. Thomas had been voted MVP of the Rose Bowl in 1939 and Vaughn had been tackle at Ole Miss. I'd heard his number called a hundred times over the radio when they were playing Alabama.

"By my count, there are at least fifteen men with real college football experience stationed in the Pacific. And I've hardly begun to look. There's no telling who I'll turn up. It strikes me as a serious oversight to have such talent handy and not make something of it. I think we need a football game."

I was washed with a vague uneasiness as I walked home. Nothing I could articulate. Just the sense that something was off kilter in the world and I was to blame for whatever it was. The rain had blown over by then and I tried not to let the uneasiness bother me, but as I passed the baseball diamond, empty now, and the row of shell-shattered abandoned buildings, busted-out windows gaping at me from across the street, whatever I was feeling began to coalesce around the idea of the lost umbrella.

Its absence had gone unnoticed, but I began to think that if I managed to retrieve it I might somehow make up for the lies I'd convinced Arthur to tell. That was the worst of it, I thought. I'd made a liar out of a little kid.

Last winter, I'd heard a story about a lieutenant in the Diplomatic Corps who'd left his coat on the back of a chair in a sake bar. He realized he'd forgotten the coat as soon as he stepped out into the cold. He went back for it right away but it was already gone. In seconds, someone had snatched it up and spirited it away. A waiter suggested that he try the *yami-ichi*. A winter coat would fetch top dollar that time of year. Technically, the black market was illegal, but it's important to understand that, without it, the locals wouldn't have been able to survive. Food was still rationed and household goods, all the ordinary items people needed to make a life, were in short supply while the factories were rebuilt or converted from military use. Even before the surrender, *yami-ichi* stalls were popping up all over Tokyo, but after a year of occupation several of these two- or three-stall clusters had grown into full blown bazaars, hundreds of vendors doing business on spread blankets and homemade tables and out of lean-tos built from scraps. Bunny knew the score. He kept the MPs away from the *yami-ichi* on the excuse that it was important for the Japanese to police themselves. And the local police were more or less indifferent. Every morning, a patrol would sweep in, round up a handful of law-breakers, and haul them off to court, where they would be processed, fined, turned loose, and back at work by afternoon. Maybe a policeman would pocket a little something for himself, but goods were rarely seized in bulk. The raids were so regular the vendors sometimes hired stand-ins to be arrested in their stead. That way, they wouldn't have to lose a day's profit or risk being robbed by a competitor while they were gone. Bunny did make it a court-martialable offense for a GI to be caught doing business on the *yami-ichi,* but the local police were afraid to bother the GIs and, before long, officers and diplomats were dispatching houseboys in search of hard-to-find items for their wives. As for the lieutenant, so the story went, he did indeed find his coat at one of the stalls. The problem was the proprietor refused to give it back. He'd paid 7000 yen for the coat, he said. He was sorry for the lieutenant but he required compensation. The lieutenant threatened to have the man arrested but they both knew he was bluffing. The story ends with the lieutenant haggling over his own coat.

The market I had in mind was located in a kind of ersatz square behind Ueno Station, the space cleared by American B-29s. It was close to the theater, the most likely place, I thought, for somebody to pawn Bunny's umbrella. You could buy almost anything, not just consumer goods—clothes, food, sundries—but industrial products as well—lumber, gasoline, fertilizer, all diverted from government supplies. There were stalls selling fish and crabs and frogs, selling stockings and perfume, selling dirty books and dirty magazines, American whiskey,

Russian vodka, cigarettes, tea leaves, jewelry; tents in which panpan girls took men between their legs next to tables offering free Bibles and tables manned by communist pamphleteers and tables set up like outdoor bars serving *katsutori soku,* selling bags of rice and grain, salvaged rubber, tatami matting, watches, record albums, record players, silverware, secondhand kimonos and school uniforms, boots, sandals, cameras, brass buttons —all of it pawned or traded by somebody in desperate need of something else, sweet potatoes, melons, live chickens, live songbirds, bricks and mortar, ink and paper, dye, bolts of cotton, spools of copper wire, candy, toys, and more and more and on and on, all the ingredients for building a new civilization at your fingertips and marked up three hundred percent. I didn't make it very deep into the market before I realized it was no use. Either the story about the lieutenant was false or he was the luckiest man alive. There was just too much ground to cover. I stood there for a long time, the market swirling around me, sound and motion and stink, the world gone dizzy in my sight, the sun disappearing behind Ueno Station, its shadow cutting like a blade down the center of the square. Then I turned and walked away and hired a rickshaw to take me home.

That night, I flinched awake from a dream about my father. In real life, he was a big man, broad-shouldered, well over six feet tall, big enough that he should have been clumsy, though he

was not. When spoken to, he had a habit of letting long pauses
hang in the air before replying. This made for awkwardness
sometimes, especially with people who didn't know him, but
he believed it was important to give due weight and consideration to whatever had been said. When I called home to tell
him I was married, there had passed a ruminant, staticky silence
before he answered, "I hope you're happy, son. There's nothing else for it now." In the dream, however, he moved in a
strange, mincing way, like a parody of a French Quarter queer,
and he spoke in rambling, high-pitched, womanish bursts that
made no sense and dissolved into hysterical laughter at the end
of every sentence. Nothing overtly frightening but the dream
brought me awake like a vision of my own death, left my heart
pounding, made the actual world seem slippery and false as my
senses put out feelers in the dark. I rubbed my eyes, blinked,
rubbed my eyes again. I picked up a familiar scent—Clifford's
foot powder, though I failed to place it right away—and in the
next instant I heard breathing and then Clifford sat up like a
vampire on his bed and I flinched again, pressing myself against
the wall.

"Jesus Christ," I said.

"Hey, buddy," Clifford said.

"What're you doing here?"

"Waiting for you to wake up."

He swung his legs to the floor and leaned forward, rest-
ing his forearms on his thighs. I couldn't see him very well but

there was a thickness to the quality of his voice that made me sure he was drunk. The moon was just a wisp outside the window, enough to graze his cheeks with light but not enough to brighten the room.

"I had the weirdest dream," I said, and when he didn't answer, I asked him, "What do you want?"

"I want to know why you're after my girl."

His voice was so calm it took a beat before I registered the meaning of his words, and then the calmness of his voice was as menacing as any sound I'd ever heard.

"What are you talking about?"

"First that business with the nigger. Now this thing with Bunny's kid. I thought you were my friend. No shit. That's how big a fool I am."

"You're crazy," I said.

"That's exactly what I been telling myself all night. Whenever I got a problem with Namiki, I said to myself, who's right there to help me out—Van is, that's who. The only married man in the whole fucking army don't cheat on his wife. And the more I kept telling myself, the fishier it sounded. Maybe I had it wrong. Maybe he's not such a nice guy. Maybe he doesn't want to fuck Fumiko. Maybe he wants to fuck somebody else. And the more I thought about it, the more it seemed like every time I turn my back on Namiki, there you are."

"Listen, Clifford—"

"Shut your mouth," he said. He scratched his chin, his neck, pushed his fingers down under the collar of his shirt to scratch his chest. He stared at me for a long moment in the dark. Then he began to weep. His crying frightened me as much as his calm, and for a few long seconds, I didn't do anything at all, just let him sob into his hands, waiting to see how all this would play out, but he kept on crying and eventually I said, "What's going on? What happened?"

He sucked in a breath, trying hard to pull himself together. "I'm losing her," he said. "Every night, she comes home smelling like GIs. I've told her to quit, but she needs the money for her family. That's what she says. She won't quit unless she can get the money some other way." He dropped his eyes, worried a hangnail on his thumb. "I keep thinking about what you said, how she's playing me, and then I start figuring she's got her eye out for a man who can give her what she needs."

"I'm an idiot," I said.

"There's ways to get the money. That's not the problem. But I don't want money to be the reason she's with me."

In the hall, somebody barefooted past our room, headed for the latrine.

"Did I ever tell you about Palawan?" Clifford said.

The answer was yes, but I figured there was a reason the story was on his mind. Clifford's tank had been part of a flying column sent out ahead of the front line to liberate an internment camp. The fighting wasn't much but it was enough to slow them down and they arrived too late. The Japs had burned the prisoners alive, rather than allow them to be rescued. Men, women, children—all of them civilians who'd been living in the Philippines before the war. "It wasn't just prisoners," Clifford said. "There were guards, too. Lined up on parade ground. Their CO called them to formation and just went on down the line— *pop, pop, pop.*" He made a pistol with his free hand and touched his index finger to his temple. I hadn't heard this part before. "It was me that found him, the CO, hiding in the closet in his office. He had the pistol in his mouth but he couldn't pull the trigger."

"What'd you do?"

Clifford said, "I put him down."

He wiped his eyes, his nose, his lips. I still wasn't sure what he would do, but all of a sudden I was too tired to be afraid.

"I'm sorry," he said.

"Don't worry about it."

"I mean it," he said. "You're a good man. I know that." He stood and began unbuttoning his shirt. "Listen, you mind if I sleep here tonight? I told Namiki off pretty good before I left."

"It's still your room," I said.

VII

I suppose I understood that nothing had been concluded with my wife, but when her next letter arrived I stood there marveling at her handwriting on the envelope, like my name and address contained a secret code, until the clerk said, "Anything else?" and I carried the letter back to the barracks to read it in my room.

I can't tell you how grateful I am to have married such a decent man and how your decency makes me ache the more, knowing I don't deserve it. I wish you were the father of this child. That may sound strange. I'm sure it is strange. But my life has been nothing if not strange these seven months. My feet are swollen and my face is all pimples. On the rare occasions when Mother can bear the sight of me, she predicts that I will have a boy because I am carrying so low. I think she's right. The baby kicks all night long. He's so stubborn. He's only ever still if I'm in motion, so I walk and walk and walk that he can rest. Mother is too ashamed to let me wander around the neighborhood so I pace the house, but that drives my father crazy when he's home. I don't mean to complain. This mess is of my own making. I know that. But it doesn't feel like a mess sometimes. I can't help falling in love with my baby even if he refuses to let me sleep. I can't help my happiness. I can't help feeling comforted by your letter. Don't misunderstand. I'll never forget the trouble I've caused. But I have one last favor to ask. Boy or girl, I'd like your permission to name the baby Francis. I'm sure that sounds strange to you as well and I'll understand if you refuse. I'll understand if you never reply to this letter at all. If that happens, I won't bother you again.

I read the letter over and over again, until I became aware that I was smiling—close-lipped and complicated but still a smile. I was remembering our first kiss. Three, maybe four seconds. I pulled away, not her. There were so many kisses after the first. Beneath the clotheslines behind her parents' house. In the back row of the Lyric. On the hood of a borrowed Ford, parked somewhere private, the radio whispering from the dashboard, the world in turmoil, the whole universe spread out over our heads.

Here, now, it was time for dinner, but the idea of sharing a table in the mess with other men, going through the motions of an ordinary night, made the muscles knot around my spine, so I folded the letter and returned it to its envelope and tucked the envelope under my pillow, inside the pillowcase, on the off chance that Clifford or somebody showed up and got curious. I headed for the street, intending to walk over to my sake bar, but on the way I changed my mind. For a few minutes, I loitered on the bench at a bus stop, nagged by hunger but without the will to help myself. Another man, local, approached and took a seat beside me and then the bus arrived, sighing and screeching like every bus in every city on the planet. The man got on and I followed him up the steps, not thinking about where I was going, thinking instead about this child who was not my child, this child who would or would not have my name. I sat next to a woman holding a pot-bellied pig. When she got off, her place was taken by another woman, about the same age, this one holding a rooster. I felt like the victim of a practical joke. For three hours, I rode that bus on an imperfect loop around the city, all the way back to where I'd boarded—through Denechofu, where Fumiko lived with her mother, and the Ichigaya district, where the International Military Tribunal conducted its affairs, and the Oimachi neighborhood, where Clifford was holed up with Namiki. Little by little, night erased the world. There were times in the army when I was glad no one had ever asked me to be a hero, and this was one. Back at the barracks, I went upstairs and closed the door and typed a letter to my wife. I told her about Bunny and Arthur. I told her about Clifford and Namiki. I told her everything that had happened to me since I first set foot in Japan. It was the longest letter I'd ever written. I told her it was all right with me if she wanted to name the baby Francis and asked her to please send me a picture when he or she was born.

There is no telling how many pages I typed during a single month in Japan. I prepared documents regarding crop yields and runaway inflation and traffic patterns and school curriculum and immunization practices and prison overcrowding. I typed an analysis of voting patterns, based on the previous election. I typed a report on "man hours lost" due to walkouts organized by the Reds and a statement from Bunny condemning "disorderly minorities." I typed more than one report on the progress of the trials. Tojo was scheduled to testify in the last week of October. Bunny wanted Arthur to bear witness—the event had significant historical value in his eyes—and Arthur wanted me to go, so Bunny cleared my schedule with Captain Embry and Ridges picked me up at the barracks and on that day I typed nothing at all.

Bunny had put the locals to work converting an auditorium at the Imperial Army Officers School into a suitable arena. Stone walls had been paneled in walnut to more closely approximate the look of an American courtroom. A long, raised, two-tiered dais was constructed for the bench—there were eleven judges altogether, each representing a victorious nation—and another smaller platform for the defendant's box directly across the room. Between them, lawyers would scuttle about on dappled marble floors imported from Torino. It was rumored that a Hollywood director had been consulted regarding where to position the media, what kind of sight lines the photographers would require, how the klieg lights should be arranged for newsreel cameras. Air conditioning and central heat had been installed, and seating was provided for a thousand spectators, half for locals, half for military and resident civilian personnel.

The gallery was full when Arthur and I arrived, but an MP in a white helmet escorted us through the crowd to the front row, where a second MP had been dispatched to save our seats. Arthur was wearing a camera around his neck. Photography was strictly forbidden in the spectators' gallery, but an exception would be made for Arthur. I was carrying his canvas satchel. In it, I knew, were legal pads, like his father's, and pencils, in case he wanted to take notes, and lunch, for both of us, packed by Mrs. Bunny. Our excursion had the air of a field trip.

Several judges were already milling around on the dais, and the lawyers, dozens of them, were in conference at wooden tables on the floor below the bench. The room rumbled with chatter. I noticed that one of the lawyers was pointing at Arthur, and another had turned to look, fifty-ish, handsome in an ordinary way, though at the moment his brow was knitted with concern. He stared at Arthur for a second, then brightened and crossed the room in our direction.

"Hey there," he said, and flashbulbs began to pop. He took Arthur's hand and shook it and held it for a moment in both of his, giving the photographers time to get a shot. "I'm glad you're here. Tell your old man I said hello."

I'd seen his face in the paper: Joseph Keenan, Chief Prosecutor, International Military Tribunal of Japan. I turned to tell Arthur who the man was but he was busy now, camera at his eye. He took pictures of the judges, the lawyers, the crowd. He took pictures as the defendants were led into the courtroom. He took pictures when a third MP rose and called the court to order, and more pictures as the Australian judge banged the room quiet with his gavel. Technically, the Australian judge was in charge, but it became clear before long that the American judge was running the show.

Tojo was seated in the front row of the defendant's box. Bald but for wisps of gray hair at the back of his skull, wearing round rimmed spectacles and a brown lapel-less suit. When Keenan called him to the stand, he pushed to his feet like the effort cost him something, then shuffled to the witness box, bowing slightly to the judges.

Keenan began by asking the witness to state his name, then led him through a series of simple questions summarizing his career from 1936 to 1945: Major General in the Imperial Army, Minister of the Imperial Army, Prime Minister of Japan.

From there, he sallied into the specifics of Tojo's role in the invasion and subsequent occupation of Manchuria, the various atrocities committed there. Tojo responded in Japanese, calmly, politely. "Such things happen in a time of war." He removed his glasses and wiped them with a handkerchief, which he kept tucked into his sleeve. "This is unfortunate but unavoidable. I was the commanding officer of the men who perpetrated the acts you have described. If in fact they did occur, then a measure of responsibility lies with me. But I issued no orders authorizing any soldier to rape any woman or murder any civilian or execute any prisoner without trial."

The proceedings moved in an awkward, halting rhythm —first Keenan, then a pause, while a translator relayed the question, then Tojo, followed by another pause, while another translator reversed the process. A few times the examination was put on hold so the judges could discuss some point of order, ruling, in each instance, in favor of the prosecution. It didn't take long for excitement to leak out of the day. By the time Keenan had steered the witness through Japan's motive for invading China and all those islands in the Pacific, each addressed methodically, individually, Japan's imperial ambition, its need for raw materials, Tojo's role in the decision-making process— by then, Arthur had put his camera down and was sketching a picture of an aircraft carrier beset by kamikazes in his pad.

"In principle," Tojo said, "it is not so different from your Monroe Doctrine."

Keenan looked at him for a moment, almost amused. In a tone so respectful as to be ironic, he said, "You're talking about principle, sir. I'm interested in facts."

"The end of war forever would require the ending of desire. This is fact."

"I suppose that depends on one's definition of the word. But now that you mention it, isn't that what we've been talking about here, sir? Japan's desire?"

Tojo shrugged. "Desire is infinite in all nations. So it is with men. War is inevitable. What is inevitable cannot be a crime."

"This tribunal begs to differ," Keenan said.

Mostly, the testimony was dry, hard to follow, names and places and dates, confirmation or denial. I had to use the head. I'd been holding it for half an hour when court finally recessed for lunch. Arthur said he didn't have to go but I couldn't leave him alone so I dragged him with me to the john. They were three deep at the trough. By the time we reached the front of the line, he was hopping from foot to foot in desperation.

Outside, the day was clear and cool, though the sun had burned the morning chill out of the air. The Tribunal was on a hilltop, and you could see the whole of Tokyo from up there, patches of greenery between the buildings in Little America and steam rising from heating units and traffic moving in the street and all around it, even now, grunge and wreckage and bare spots on the cityscape where entire blocks had been obliterated.

We sat on the steps outside the auditorium to eat our peanut butter and jelly sandwiches, our celery and apples. Several vendors had set up shop and spectators were scattered at intervals on the steps. Farther down, kept at bay by more white-helmeted MPs, a group of protesters strolled in lazy rectangles, wearing signboards and carrying banners on long poles. I recognized one of the men, his moles and his mustache. From the sake bar. The man I'd seen with Clifford and Eguchi. He was wearing a signboard with Japanese characters on one side and what I assumed was its translation, in English, on the other.

Imperial Edict:
The national polity has been maintained.
I am eating my fill,
you people starve and die.
—Imperial sign and seal

I watched him—up three steps, across, down three steps, and back again.

"This is boring," Arthur said.

"No argument here."

"Can we leave?"

"We've made it this far."

"Please," he said. "Please, Van."

I said, "I know your dad would like it if we stuck around," and the mention of his father settled the matter. I felt sorry for him. Stifled. Disappointed. Without recourse. A day so full of promise had dissolved into tedium, the end nowhere in sight.

"Who do you think would win," I asked Arthur, "in a fight between John Wayne and a ninja?"

Arthur stopped a celery stick an inch from his lips.

"Would they have weapons?"

"I think not."

"Would the fight be organized—you know, like a boxing match—or would it be like the ninja jumped him in an alley or something?"

"Which would be more interesting, do you think?"

It was a complicated question, warranting serious consideration. For a few minutes, we debated the rules of engagement and if John Wayne would fight in character or as himself. I could tell Arthur was trying to steer the variables in John Wayne's favor. Even so, he was having a tough time arriving at a scenario where an actor would have the advantage over an assassin.

"You can't discount the intangibles," I told him. "John Wayne's got guts. There's no quit in John Wayne."

Arthur crunched his celery, unconvinced.

"Maybe the trial will pick up after lunch," I said, but after lunch was more of the same. Keenan did eventually get around to Pearl Harbor, but by then, Arthur had dozed off with his head on my bicep, leaking drool onto my sleeve. No matter what Keenan asked, Tojo replied as though all of this had been settled long before he took the stand. He seemed a little bored himself as Keenan pressed him about the War Rescript and the deliberation leading up to the Pearl Harbor and who was involved and on what grounds and how had the decision been reached to attack without issuing a declaration of war.

Tojo rubbed his eyes, sighed. The answer was obvious.

"We would have lost the element of surprise," he said.

"Are you aware that the Emperor himself has condemned the attack on Pearl Harbor? According to Emperor Hirohito, he didn't know what you had planned until he read about it in the paper."

"I am aware of those statements. I am also aware that the Emperor has not been called to testify before this tribunal." Tojo looked at the ranks of reporters as he spoke, and what came next was the nearest thing to a dramatic moment that afternoon.

"Objection," Keenan said.

One of the lawyers at the defense table pushed to his feet. "He can't object to the testimony of his own witness, your honor."

Without conferring with the rest of the bench, the American judge said, "The witness's last remark will be stricken from the record."

The defense attorney started to protest but the judge held up his hand. "The record will reflect your objection but not the witness's statement. That's it, counsel. Not another word."

He turned to Tojo. "And you, sir, will restrict your testimony to answering the questions that have been asked."

Tojo linked his fingers in his lap and dropped his eyes. Quietly, in English, he said, "I will be hanged in any case."

The American judge snatched the gavel out of the Australian's hand and banged it, once, twice, then pointed it at Tojo. "I assure you, sir, that's not the way we do business. You will be punished only if that man there proves your guilt. Now, will you behave or do I need to have you removed from court? Understand that if you are removed, evidence against you will be read into the record and neither you nor your attorney will have the opportunity for rebuttal."

"I will answer your questions," Tojo said.

And so they went on, through Luzon and Bataan, and was it true that Tojo ordered such and such at such and such a time, and afterward, in the car on the way home, Arthur asked me, "What did I miss?" His eyes were bleary, his cheeks lined from the wrinkles in my shirt.

"Not a thing," I said.

"Don't tell my dad, OK?"

"Don't tell him what?"

"That I fell asleep."

I pinched two fingers together and drew them over my lips like I was pulling a zipper closed and I let myself wonder about the possibility that this child who would have my name might turn out to be a boy. It occurs to me now, typing these words, that that moment, with Arthur at my side, the Packard rounding Hibiya Park, so familiar after so much time—the footpaths and the moat and the leafless cherry trees—but still exotic in its way, still able to kindle in me a sense of how far I'd come from everything I'd ever known—it occurs to me that that was my last happy moment in Japan.

VIII

Twenty-seven hours after Ridges dropped me at the barracks and delivered Arthur safely home, Clifford and Namiki checked into a small resort hotel in Kamakura. Clifford sent the innkeeper for sake like they were on their honeymoon. They slept late in the morning. Took breakfast in bed at Clifford's insistence, followed by a walk on the beach, deserted, I imagine, at that time of year, the ocean wide and black and cold, waves rolling in exactly as they'd rolled in forever, wind bending the seagrass and brushing sand up from the dunes. In the afternoon, they visited the local Shinto shrine and offered a donation so that the novitiates would dance a blessing on their love. On their second night in Kamakura, at approximately 2200 hours, Clifford shot himself in the temple with his sidearm, then Namiki turned the pistol on herself. The innkeeper and his wife were awakened by the noise.

I wasn't there of course. I witnessed none of the above. The reason I'm in possession of particulars at all is that two days later, I woke and made my bed, showered, shaved, the whole business so habitual I stumbled through it half-awake, but on this morning a Major Charlie Roebuck of the Criminal Investigations Division was waiting for me when I got back to my room.

I was wearing only a towel. He smiled like he was glad to see me. I noticed a divot in his neck where some shrapnel had been removed.

"If I'm not mistaken, you're PFC Francis Vancleave, but everybody calls you Van."

"Yessir."

"Tell you what, Van, why don't you put some clothes on and we'll head over to my office. I've got a few questions for you and I'd rather not do this here if I can help it."

He rubbed the top of his head. Crewcut. He could have worn it longer if he wanted. This was peace time. The army didn't care.

"What's this about, sir?"

"Let's discuss all that at my place if you don't mind."

"What about work?"

"Don't you worry," he said. "That's all taken care of."

He leaned in the doorway with his back to me while I dressed, speaking now and then to the other men passing in the hall, like his presence was nothing unusual, no cause for alarm.

CID was housed in what had been a bank before the war. The building was only a couple of blocks from the barracks but Roebuck insisted we take his car. The city yawned and stretched and shivered itself awake around us. He set me up in an interview room—table, two chairs, walls painted marine surplus gray—then ducked out for a few minutes and when he returned, he had a manila folder tucked under his arm.

"When was the last time you saw your roommate?"

"I'm not sure, sir. Maybe two weeks."

Roebuck opened the folder and pushed a photograph in my direction. As part of an ongoing campaign, he told me, CID had raided the apartment of a poet known to be a communist sympathizer. He tapped the photograph. "We didn't expect to turn up any contraband," he said. "Every so often, we just like to remind the Reds that the army's paying attention." But they did find something—a single crate of Browning Automatic Rifles. "Not enough to restart the war, but enough to cause plenty of trouble." The BARs were traced back to the Battalion Armory in Tokyo. CID arrested the first sergeant in charge of inventory, and he rolled on Clifford right away. He claimed he had no idea what happened to the rifles after they left his warehouse. If he'd known the BARs were going to wind up in communist hands, he said, he would never have gone along with Clifford's plan.

"Course nobody believes him." Roebuck fingered the divot in his neck. "He's just trying to get out in front of his own court-martial. Who can blame him? But we've only got his testimony and he's put all the weight on your buddy Clifford Price."

I recognized the poet. Mustache, moles. The photograph was taken at night. Hard to tell where. But there was no mistaking the identity of the other person in the picture.

"Your houseboy muled the rifles," Roebuck said.

Both of them were in custody at Sugamo Prison. Neither, according to Roebuck, would ever see the light of day again.

"Most likely, it was this Eguchi who tipped your roommate."

Clifford had managed to clear out before CID could pick him up. Didn't bother covering his tracks. He wasn't really trying to escape. CID had no trouble tracing his movements. They had statements from the innkeeper and his wife and from several guests at the hotel. They'd interviewed the novitiates at the shrine. It was unclear how much Namiki knew about the rifles. What could be presumed, however, was that she had chosen to take her life. Roebuck showed me the crime scene photos. Her body slumped over his. Blood pooled like a shadow.

"We suspected murder-suicide," Roebuck said, "but the paraffin test indicates otherwise. Plus there's the position of the bodies."

I opened my mouth to ask a question, but no sound came out. My vision had gone blurry at the edges. I cleared my throat to find my voice.

"What's all this got to do with me, sir?"

"Clifford Price arranged your initial invitation to the MacArthurs' residence, isn't that right?"

"Yessir."

"Was it his idea to buy Arthur MacArthur a birthday present?"

"Nosir."

"Explain it to me then. Why does a typist buy a birthday present for a general's kid?"

"I felt sorry for him, I guess."

"You felt sorry for him?"

"He's lonely," I said. "He's eight years old."

Roebuck said, "Well, aren't you a decent human being," and I understood then that he was sniffing around for a conspiracy. As if the tumult of Clifford's love wasn't motive enough. I shouldn't have been surprised—in those days, everybody was anxious about the Reds—but my heart lurched at the thought.

"Arthur is my friend," I said and even as I spoke the words, I could hear how ridiculous, how pathetic they sounded, but that didn't make them any less the truth.

Roebuck frowned and scraped his chair back, the sound loud enough to make me jump, and left me in the interview room alone. He was gone for hours. I tried the knob, but it was locked. I paced and tried the knob again and yet again, pressed my ear to the door, heard nothing. The silence beyond the door was total. Like I was the only person left in the building. Like I was buried deep under the earth.

Finally, he reappeared and said, "I guess I know where to find you if we have more questions," and just like that he cut me loose.

* * *

The day was beginning to fade by the time I emerged, one of those enormous Japanese moons asserting its place prematurely in the sky. I wasn't sure what to do with myself. It was too late to report for duty and I couldn't bear the thought of answering the questions that were coming. I didn't know how to answer them besides. Roebuck had said nothing about confidentiality, but I felt in possession of a terrible secret. I tucked my chin into my collar and hurried back to the barracks, an American flag snapping in the breeze atop nearly every building on the way.

Had I ever seen the barracks so abandoned? I wandered the halls, peeking into rooms, every bed made to pass inspection. No matter how orderly, grown men in close quarters will produce an oily, musty tang. I'd been living with that smell for so long I'd ceased to notice it, but it came back to me now in waves. When I heard the voices of men returning from work, I holed up in my room, listened to the barracks buzzing and creaking around me, the sound muted, distant. It wasn't long before Rudy Grand knocked on my door.

"Where were you all day?"

"Nowhere."

"Don't be an ass," he said. "That guy was CID."

I just kept looking at him. He was holding a deck of cards.

"Wanna play a little gin?" he said.

"No, thanks."

"I'll spot you points."

I said, "No, thanks," again, and he turned to go but this idea popped into my head.

"You wouldn't have a Bible by any chance?"

Rudy shrugged and headed off in the direction of his room, came back bearing a battered King James. When he was gone, I flipped pages until I found the Sermon on the Mount. *Consider the lilies of the field* and *Do not give unto dogs what is holy* and so forth. I read that over a few times, then skipped around to other passages like I might find some answers, but none of what I read made me feel better about anything.

Reports of Clifford's death made the rounds but I kept my mouth shut on the subject, and for the most part people left me alone. I was the known associate of a traitor. I'd been interrogated by CID. My roommate had offed himself. All of which added up to as wide a berth as I desired.

Bunny's note arrived on Friday, delivered to my desk by one of his many aides.

Your Saturday obligation is hereby terminated.

Handwritten on official SCAP stationery. Signed by Bunny himself. Just six words, but I knew exactly what he meant. At first, I blamed Mrs. Bunny. She'd made it clear that she did not approve of me, and for a few foolish minutes I considered storming up to Bunny's office to protest. But I knew it was no use. He wouldn't contradict his wife on my behalf, and the truth is I couldn't blame either of them for wanting to put some distance between me and their son. As swiftly and awkwardly as I'd been ushered into Arthur's life, I'd been shown the door, guilty by association.

That night, unable to sleep, I made up my mind to go looking for the room Clifford had shared with Namiki. I'm not sure what I hoped to find, but the idea that I might find something proved impetus enough. I knew the room was in the Oimachi neighborhood and Clifford had mentioned a bathhouse nearby. I figured I could take the bus out there, ask directions to the bathhouse and maybe somebody at the bathhouse could point me toward the lodgings of the American corporal and his *onri wan*. Which is exactly what happened. I set out on Saturday at the hour I'd normally have been headed for the residence. The bus driver told me where to find the bathhouse, and an attendant at the bathhouse knew where Clifford lived.

He gave me a landmark to look for—a bomb crater, twenty feet across, filled with rainwater and deep enough that in all this time the sun had failed to bake it dry. Four boys were horsing around in the water when I arrived. Naked. Shivering from the cold of it. I knocked at what I hoped was the right house and an old woman answered the door, her face as wrinkled as a crumpled paper sack.

"Your girl here," she said, as if she'd been expecting me. "You rent room."

I tried to explain who I was and that I just wanted to poke around, but she was insistent.

"She here. Nice face. One week two dollar."

With her apron, the old woman shooed me across the patch of dirt that passed for a yard. The entrance to Clifford's room was off the alley behind the house, and as I rounded the corner I heard her start in on those boys. Her Japanese was too fast for me to follow, but I could guess what she was saying. *Put some clothes on. Keep your voices down. Where are your mothers? That water isn't clean.* What old women say to boys.

The alley was hung with laundry down the length of it. Another house backed up to this one, and so on down the line. There was an old-fashioned bike with a big front tire leaning against the wall. Clifford's door was open. Inside, a second woman, much younger, was sorting through a basket of what I presumed were Namiki's clothes, and I understood the landlady's mistake. She assumed we were together. I could make out the rim of this woman's ear where it peeked up through her hair, the line of her jaw where the hair draped away from her face. Without making my presence known, I watched her select a slip from the basket and carry it over to a chipped and blurry mirror on the wall. She held the slip against her body, pinning it in place under her chin and smoothing the silk with both hands. Her left arm was white to the elbow with scar tissue. What looked like burns had curled her hand into a claw.

"Fumiko?" I said, and she whirled to face me, hiding her burned hand behind her back. She started jabbering in Japanese. I was pretty sure she was trying to convince me that she had permission to take the clothes.

"I don't care," I said.

Wide-eyed, still uncertain, Fumiko nodded and I stepped inside. This room had suffered in the air raids. Two of the original walls were intact but the other two were cobbled together with roofing tin and salvaged wood, some kind of putty in the seams. The planks of the floor were mismatched, the gaps between them wide enough in places that you could see through to the dusty, shadowy region under the house, a kingdom of rats and spiders. A bare bulb dangled from the ceiling. Cold seeped in from everywhere. But the room was clean and the futon was draped with mosquito netting in a way that looked exotic. By way of decoration, advertisements had been clipped from American magazines and tacked up on the walls. Pretty young housewives pushing New Brite mops and washing pots and pans in Bon Ami. Movie stars would have been one thing, but for some reason the sight of all those beaming women engaged in such ordinary tasks left me reeling. I flopped back on the futon. Through the mosquito netting, Fumiko looked wavery and indistinct.

"What happened to your hand?" I said, and she said, "Bomu," in a voice bored with answering that question, and I wondered if she blamed Tojo and company or us. She spoke again in Japanese. It took a moment to process what she'd said. A letter. He'd left a letter. I swung myself upright and brushed the mosquito net aside.

"Where?"

Fumiko pointed at a table and there it was—not a suicide note, not an explanation or apology, but his weekly letter to his mother, forgotten, I guessed, in the scramble to skip town.

For once, Mother Dear, I have real news. Your Clifford has got himself a girl. She's beautiful and smart and I know you'll like her even though she's Japanese. Don't panic, sweetheart. This is not your ordinary Jap. She works as a model in a department store and she loves everything American. She won't even eat rice anymore—too Japanese! Her name is Namiki and I've been seeing her for a while. I wanted to tell you about her the day we met but I needed to be sure of everything before I wrote. I remember the stories you used to tell about how Dad chased you for so long and how you never loved him and then one day something changed and suddenly you did. I knew I loved Namiki right away and now I know she loves me too, and you better get used to the idea because I intend to bring her home.

I figured Fumiko would want to know what the letter said but the idea of piecing together some kind of translation made me tired. She was standing at my back, watching me, waiting. I felt like I owed her something. I closed my eyes for a second, then folded the letter into a square, tucked it in my hip pocket, and offered her Eguchi's job.

IX

When we first arrived in Tokyo, fourteen months before, all enlisted men assigned to the Occupation were required to watch a film called *Our Job in Japan*. The film had been produced by the War Department, and its purpose was to go beyond fear and propaganda and educate us on the nature of the locals. I hadn't paid much attention, to tell the truth. That was September, and the room was warm enough to make you drowsy. It was like one of those days when you got to watch a film strip in grade school—a pleasant change of pace but boring nevertheless. What I remembered most about the film was the image of a hovering cartoon brain and the narrator's voice assuring us that, scientifically speaking, the Japanese brain was just like ours, composed of the exact same tissues, firing with the same electrical impulses. Feed any brain negative data, like tyranny and oppression, and it will lead to negative behavior like Pearl Harbor and Bataan. That's what the narrator said. Feed it positive data, like democracy and freedom, and positive results, like going to church and donating to charity and so forth, will inevitably follow. Our job in Japan was to nourish the Japanese brain with the example of our kindness, with our innate American decency.

The image of that brain came back to me in the weeks following Clifford's death, with winter creeping in, alone in the quiet darkness of my room. I saw this brain like a luminous purple sponge behind my eyes, and I tried to convince myself that surely Fumiko was grateful for the opportunity I'd provided, that I was supplying a positive example with my thoughtfulness and generosity, just as the narrator had instructed, but then I'd picture her on her knees in the empty barracks, working a scrub brush around a commode, and it was hard to feel entirely affirmed. Twice a week, Fumiko rode her bike out to the barracks. Tuesdays and Fridays. I had no trouble convincing the men. Eguchi was in jail and nobody else had come up with a replacement. Fumiko even took in mending on the side for extra cash. Leave your frayed-cuff pants or your hole-y socks on the foot of your bed and they would vanish, only to reappear a few days later good as new. Most mornings, we had reported for duty by the time she showed up, and by the time we got home she'd already pedaled off into the night. It was like sharing the building with a fastidious ghost.

So I'd picture her scrubbing the john or darning socks in the dim light of the room she shared with her mother, and I'd start thinking about my own brain, all the data I'd received in my whole life, what kind of person I'd become as a result. And then other brains would come floating up as well, these cartoon brains looming inside my own. I wondered about my wife's brain and Arthur MacArthur's brain and Bunny's brain, but my wondering always looped back around to Clifford and Namiki. I'd picture their brains side by side, lit up like control panels, gauges flickering, monitors blinking, the great red warning lights of their love, and I'd try to imagine the precise combination of data that led them to do what they had done. I understood the basics. It was easy enough to grasp the motivation behind Clifford's crime and I believed he had committed it, despite my fondness for him, and I could imagine the desperation he must have felt, that both of them had felt, when it became apparent that Clifford would be caught. But that's just information. That's just raw data. The act itself failed to compute.

Eventually, my brain would wear itself out and I'd sag backward into sleep and then it would be morning, light streaming in through the window like nothing terrible ever happened in the world. I'd roll out of bed and hit the showers and shuffle off to another day of typing while Fumiko made the barracks clean.

I avoided the mess hall after Clifford's death. I didn't mind the gossip and the looks. What I couldn't bear was sympathy. I took meals at my sake bar instead. I'd drink too much and wonder if Clifford had ever considered me his friend, if he'd ever considered me at all except when I could be of service. I told myself it didn't make sense for me to be so thrown.

One morning, a Friday, a few weeks before Thanksgiving, I slept through reveille for the first time since I'd joined up. I came to, wistful with hangover. I registered the quiet and the quality of the light on the walls, somehow thinner than usual, and the back of my neck went prickly. I snatched my watch up off the table, but I already knew I was late. Ten minutes later, I was taking the stairs three at a time while simultaneously tucking in my shirt and combing my fingers through my hair when I met Fumiko as she climbed. Her eyes widened as I came barreling toward her and she pressed herself against the wall. She was carrying a broom and mop over her right shoulder, an old ten-gallon paint bucket in her left—her burned—hand. In the bucket, she carried wash rags and scrub brushes and bottles of whatever local potion she used to rid the barracks of our smell. She was wearing *monpe* pantaloons. She had a bandanna tied over her hair. I took note of all this even as I missed a step and lost my balance and careened into the air. The next thing I knew I was curled up on the landing, bleeding from a gash at my hairline and Fumiko was beside me, asking if I was all right in Japanese. Her face was very close. I noticed that her eyebrows were thick and black, set off by the paleness of her skin. She wiped the blood from my forehead with her bad hand.

"I'm fine," I said. "Thank you. *Arigato*. I'm OK."

I pushed to my feet and patted myself all over to be sure. I felt a little woozy and the cut was deep enough that I needed

a trip to the infirmary, but otherwise I thought I would survive. Fumiko took a step away from me and slipped her bad
hand into her sleeve. Both of us were embarrassed. I offered to
help her carry her supplies, but she refused, so I stood there at
a loss while she gathered her things and climbed the stairs without looking back, the paint bucket swinging against her leg.

The following Tuesday, with seven stitches in my brow, I
dawdled over my coffee and my shave until everyone had left
for work. I kept a vigil on the street from the window in my
room. I watched Fumiko lean her bike against the building,
then counted to a hundred in my head, trying to give her
enough time to collect her supplies from the storage closet in
the basement. Finally, I headed for the stairs, slowly this time.
When Fumiko saw me coming, she said, "*Ohayo,*" and stepped
aside to let me pass. I replied in kind and continued on my way
and that was all.

At the OPS, Captain Embry razzed me for being late but
didn't make as big a stink as he could have, and for the rest of
the day I banged out pages for the army. Nothing had changed.
But I felt somehow as if it had. This change was neither good
nor bad, but I took a kind of comfort in it just the same.

I repeated this routine on Friday and again on Tuesday
and each time my interaction with Fumiko was the same. At
the end of the week, Captain Embry called me into his office

and offered me a chair and shut the door behind us. He took a seat behind the desk, rubbed his face with both hands, his cheek bulging with tobacco.

"Well." He gave me a sympathetic smile. "I guess I should have called you in a while back but I figured you needed . . . room."

I kept my mouth shut while he fidgeted.

"How you holding up?" he said.

"Fine, sir."

"Good," he said. "The only thing to do is put your head down and march."

"Yessir."

"Listen, you know I'm no hardass. I'm an insurance sales-man. But I can't let you keep going on the way you been. It's not fair to the others."

He tipped his chin in the direction of the door.

"I understand, sir," I said.

"If you're late again," he said, "I'm going to have to write you up."

"Yessir."

"All right, then," he said.

"Can I ask you a question, sir?"

"Shoot."

"What happens to the bodies?"

His face fell. It looked like he'd swallowed his chew.

"The what?"

"Of military criminals. I've been wondering what they do with the bodies."

"Hell, son, I don't know. I guess they send em home like all the rest."

"That's what I thought," I said.

For Thanksgiving, 300 turkeys were shipped alive to Tokyo by a patriotic poultryman in Oklahoma, and a number of these arrived in the mess hall at the Imperial Finance Ministry, dressed, of course, soaked all night in brine, burnished now and glistening from the ovens, somehow unruined by cooks whose talents ran more naturally to stew. The men were allotted three cans of beer apiece, and the meal was supplemented by canned cranberry sauce from the PX and rice grown in Japan and brown gravy, which the cooks had no trouble whipping up. Brown gravy was a specialty of the house. It should have been a pleasant afternoon and I suppose it was for most of the men, but I took one look at all that food laid out on the tables, felt all those voices washing over me, and retreated to my sake bar.

Plenty of locals were bustling about. Maybe an hour of daylight left. I thought about Fumiko as I walked, her eyebrows, her earlobes, the touch of her fingers on my brow, and I wondered if the locals had a holiday like Thanksgiving. And then I wondered if one day there would be a Japanese holiday commemorating their liberation by the powerful but bighearted Americans, all the blessings thus entailed.

As I neared my sake bar, I passed the panpan girls on their stoops. The night wouldn't get busy for hours yet, and a few of them still had curlers in their hair. The boys that worked the street like carnival barkers—*Hey hey, GI, you meet my sister?*—were knotted around a barrel fire on the sidewalk, voices rising and falling like grown men. Not one of them bothered to ask if I was interested in a girl.

The sake bar was empty but for the waitress. I took a seat and gave her my order and watched the boys on the street. The tallest one brought a fist up to his mouth and moved his lips. I thought it looked like he was singing, the fist holding an imaginary microphone. He was maybe twelve, thirteen years old. The others were laughing at him—appreciatively, it seemed. The waitress returned with a *katakuchi* of sake, and I downed a cup fast enough that I could feel the heat of it in my stomach, then another, then a third. I left a handful of scrip on the counter and walked back outside. The tallest kid, the singer, stepped away from the others at my approach.

"How come you never ask me to meet your sister anymore?" I said.

"I ask you hundred times."

"What about tonight?"

"You meet my sister?"

"Which one's your sister?"

"Which you want?"

I looked over at the girls. There was one with marcel waves in her hair, holding a cigarette with her wrist cocked. She seemed apart from the others, knees together in a prim and proper way, free hand in her lap.

I pointed and he said, "That my sister."

He called to her in Japanese. The girl hung the cigarette between her lips and ticked toward us on her heels.

"What's your name?" I said.

"What name you like?"

I thought about it for a second.

"Fumiko," I said.

The singer hitched his eyebrows as if surprised that I'd requested a Japanese name, but then he shrugged—he'd heard stranger things—and said, "This lucky day, GI. Her name Fumiko."

The girl popped a button on her blouse, third from the top, took my hand, and guided it under her shirt, cupped my palm over her breast. She wasn't wearing a bra. She closed her eyes, shuddered. She dragged on her cigarette. Her breast was small, her nipple hard in the cold. I could feel her heartbeat, the goosebumps on her skin. We stayed like that for twelve beats of her heart; then I said, "Happy Thanksgiving," and withdrew my hand and walked away. The singer started in on me in an extravagant mix of English and Japanese, cursing me, telling me he knew I was a waste of time, knew I only buggered other men. I'd gone half a block when he came trotting up behind me.

"You got gum?" he said. "You got chocolate?"

He was all smiles now.

"Not tonight," I said.

In December, Bunny commenced the preparations for his football game. He transferred three dozen soldiers, all with college football experience, from various assignments in the Pacific to the Special Services branch of his command, divided them into teams, and set them to practicing. He wasn't after some sandlot deal. He wanted something inspiring, something symbolic. To this end, he chose Hiroshima for the site. "Here occurred the single greatest act of destruction in the history of man," he said, in one of many press releases on the subject, "and now it will showcase man's infinite capacity for healing." The paperwork was a landslide and every page had to be completed on the double, so the OPS was buried. A full company of engineers was assigned to shore up the old stone grandstand at a former equestrian center, to build a scoreboard, bleachers, goalposts. Local children were enlisted to crawl on their hands and knees, picking shards of glass and rubble from the field. Uniforms were designed. Equipment flown in from the states. The Marine Brass Band dispatched. Not a detail overlooked by Bunny. If everything went according to plan, the Tokyo Giants would kick off to the Hiroshima Bears at precisely noon on New Year's Day, 1947, in the Atom Bowl—so dubbed by Bunny himself.

As a reward for our hard work, all the typists in the OPS were issued a pair of tickets to the game, and because I didn't want to go alone, because I felt cast off by everything that had happened, I decided to invite Fumiko. As on those other mornings, I lingered in the barracks until the rest of the men were gone, until I saw Fumiko rolling up the street, hair breezing out behind her like a cape. I wasn't concerned about Captain Embry. Maybe he'd write me up, but that was no big deal.

Two weeks had passed since I last greeted Fumiko on the stairs and I worried, at the sight of her, that invititing her might be a mistake. I slipped by along the railing, intending to let her go about her business, then my heart started pounding and I changed my mind again a few steps farther down. I stopped, blurted, "Have you ever heard of football?" and Fumiko frowned at me over her shoulder. Of course she hadn't heard of football. It took a few minutes and a muddle of English and Japanese, but I managed to convey the notion that I planned to attend an American sporting event and would be pleased if she would join me. She dropped her eyes, studied her feet. She nodded, just once, crisply, and we arranged to meet at Ueno Station on the morning of the game.

* * *

I waited for her in the predawn dark, my thoughts still murky with sleep, the platform teeming with GIs, their voices too loud, too jovial at that hour. I recognized some of the men but didn't feel like speaking, and everybody kept their distance. It was cold and all the lights were ringed with yellow haze. Bunny had arranged a series of direct trains to Hiroshima for the purpose of shuttling spectators to the game. He wanted to be sure there was a crowd, plenty of witnesses. I'd typed several memos on the subject. The first train had left the night before and ours was to be the last. I was beginning to think Fumiko would stand me up when she appeared in the doorway between the station house and the platform. The first thing I noticed was her coat, heavy wool, motley with patches, but as my eyes traveled the length of her, I saw a few inches of dress below the hem. Red with white polka dots. Nylons smoothing her shins. Namiki's hand-me-downs.

"Fumiko!"

I waved and pressed toward her through the crowd and she bowed with her hands tucked into her sleeves.

"Thank you very much for this gracious invitation."

Her English sounded memorized, like she'd been practicing the line.

We found our seats, waited for the ticket agent to come around. Fumiko had the window. With dawn nudging the sky, the city gave way to open fields, a ridge of mountains on the horizon. We trestled over a river, then over it again an hour down the line. This was beautiful country, even dulled by winter. I wanted to give Fumiko a sense of what we were about to see but my Japanese was too rudimentary and her English even worse and there exists no translation for words like quarterback and touchdown. We lapsed into silence while all around us men were jawing and roughhousing and roaming the aisles. Behind me, I heard someone say, "Pass me that there hooch," and someone else said, "But if you *had* a thousand dollars?" and up ahead of me, I heard, "Bill Bertelli scored five touchdowns against Syracuse in '39."

Just after Kyoto it started snowing, flakes darting like schools of fish outside the windows. We passed through a village untouched by war. Little houses. Chimney smoke. A dog chasing the train. Skinny enough that you could make out his ribs and hipbones and the knobs of his spine, but even so he was really getting after it, tongue hanging out, ears pinned back, his whole body in the chase.

"Fast," I said, and Fumiko smiled.

"Thank you very much," she said, "for this gracious invitation."

Eventually, the train passed into a wintry forest and then out onto the plain around Hiroshima. Fumiko leaned her brow against the window, her breath misting the glass. I took in the scene over her shoulder. The world bulldozed. A scrap of metal. A hunk of concrete. A man alone. Difficult to imagine that anything had ever existed in this place until you noticed the scorched and gutted hulks of buildings big enough to survive the blast rising like weird barnacles on the landscape. Until you noticed that the man was walking on a road, wind lifting snow from the pavement and setting it to dance, and the road he was on linked up with other roads, leading nowhere now. The view was deceptive. The bomb hadn't done all that damage. Heavy machinery had helped. An effort had been made to scrape away the evidence of destruction, to make way for something new. The bomb got the ball rolling. The wheels of progress had done the rest. But in that first moment, a hush descended on the train and everybody held their breath.

The silence began to lift as we came into the station. Here was the Red Cross hospital. The noodle shop. *Yami-ichi* vendors lined up on the street despite the cold. Panpan girls. The buildings were new, wood-frame, temporary-looking. All around us men hooted with laughter and swigged from whiskey-filled canteens and bumped shoulders as they walked. Everybody was trying hard to shake off that first impression. I steered Fumiko along in the stream of bodies, trusting the momentum of the crowd to lead us, and she huddled close against my side.

As we entered the stadium, a soldier manning the gate asked where I was stationed, then handed me a program and a Tokyo Giants pennant. Turned out the teams had been divided between those men assigned to units in and around Tokyo, where the Occupation was concentrated, and those out in the provinces or at sea. The grandstand was full, but we hunted up seats in the bleachers across the field. The crowd was mostly GIs, but there were a fair number of locals present as well, most of them standing in the open spaces beyond either endzone but a few, like Fumiko, were scattered in the stands. Women. The guests of soldiers. Down on the field, the players were stretching, passing the ball around. Calvin Thomas had been selected captain of the Bears, Bill Bertelli of the Giants, and both were allowed to fill out their rosters with players from among the ranks of regular GIs, guys who'd played a little ball in high school, enough of them that the scene had the look of an honest-to-God pregame warm-up. I spotted Bill Bertelli on the bench, smoking a cigarette, wrapped in an army-issue blanket. I started to point him out for Fumiko, but I knew it was no use. Snow wisped down and melted in her hair. The sky was like an old white bowl turned upside down over our heads. We were sitting on the second row from the top of the bleachers and I counted down fourteen rows to the sideline then started to count the heads across the row in front of us, trying to estimate how many people were in the stands, but I was distracted by a murmur running through the crowd. The MacArthurs were making their entrance at the gate, surrounded by officers, dignitaries, the whole entourage ringed with MPs, Bunny in the middle of it all with his pipe clenched between his teeth. I could just make out the top of Arthur's head. Bunny accompanied his family into the grandstand, kissed his wife, tousled Arthur's hair, then descended to a podium on the sideline. His speech was later reprinted in half the newspapers in the world.

"I address you today on behalf of those voices forever silenced in the jungles and on the beaches and in the deep waters of the Pacific and on behalf of the thousands upon thousands who perished in an instant in this place. Make no mistake that a terrible thing happened here—at once the pinnacle of man's intellectual achievement and his capacity for self-annihilation. The forces of democracy were called upon to make an appalling choice but, in making that choice, obliterated the edifice of tyranny, leaving the world unshadowed, the sun no longer dimmed by oppression. Today, unshackled peoples are tasting the sweetness of freedom, the relief from fear. We stand on the threshold of a new life. What vast panoramas will open before us none can say. They are there, just beyond the horizon, just there, and they are of a magnificence and diversity far beyond the comprehension of anyone present on this occasion. Together, we celebrate not only the dawning of a new year but of a new world, a world without boundaries, a world whose limits will be as broad as the spirit and the imagination of man himself. Of all men. I thank merciful God for giving us the faith and courage to achieve victory and for turning our minds toward lasting peace. I ask Him to watch over those who take the field today, to keep them safe from injury, and to grace this remarkable event with His presence."

He paused, one beat, two. I glanced at Arthur. Even from this distance, I could see how he was looking at his father, and

I thought it must have seemed like all of this had been organized just for him.

In a casual, almost confidential voice, Bunny added, "We all know the Lord loves football. I expect He's found Himself a seat. If not, somebody please make room."

Then he saluted the crowd and the Marine Band launched into "Glory Hallelujah" and the players trotted out and suddenly the ball was in the air, the Giants kicking to the Bears in the city of Hiroshima, on the island of Honshu, in the occupied nation of Japan.

The game itself went back and forth. Tokyo moved into the lead behind the running of Bill Bertelli. The man was a mule. Most plays it took three or four tacklers to bring him down. In the early going, despite the speech and the pageantry and the frills, the game felt exactly like what it was, an exhibition, the players showing off and having fun, the crowd responding with whistles and applause, but it was obvious Bill Bertelli wanted to win. He lowered his shoulder every time he had the ball and beat a path through the snow, and gradually something began to change. Hiroshima was trailing by two touchdowns at the end of the first quarter but scored on a reverse early in the second, Calvin Thomas arching around behind the line and racing fifty-odd yards to the end zone. They scored again, two possessions later, on a long pass from Dante Pasquali, who'd backed up a Heisman Trophy winner at Notre Dame. And as the clock ticked down the second quarter, I had the sense that each toss sweep was half a step faster than before, the tackles more reckless, the crowd growing more frantic and intense. The bleachers trembled beneath our feet. Late in the half, when Bill Bertelli was upended on a dive over the middle, when he landed on his back just shy of a first down, I found myself leaping from my seat with everybody else and letting loose a howl.

At halftime, the Marine Band marched out onto the field playing "On Wisconsin." I guess they figured any fight song would do. When they were finished, a chorus of local children sang "God Bless America" in English. Their voices were so sweet, so high and awkward and pure. Fumiko brought a hand up to wipe her eyes and I could see that she'd been crying. I asked her what was wrong and she said, "Thank you very much for this gracious invitation," then pushed to her feet and picked her way through the stands, headed for the exit. I started to follow but the second half was about to begin and the game was tied and I didn't want to miss anything. I told myself that maybe she wanted to be alone.

The GI on my left tapped my ankle with his boot and said, "That's too bad, buddy." He'd been tapping my ankle all day long, saying things like, "Get a load of that, buddy," or "How bout that, buddy," drawing my attention to certain plays like I wasn't sitting beside him watching the game myself. He had a stocking cap pulled down low over his brow. The cap made his head look too small for his shoulders.

"What's too bad?" I said.

"Your girl there."

"What about her?"

"Well, she left, didn't she?"

"She's not my girl," I said.

"She's not your girl? Then what'd you bring her for?"

I could feel the pulse thumping in my neck.

"She's a student of the game," I said.

The GI coughed up a laugh.

"I'll bet, buddy. I'll bet she's a student of the game."

When the third quarter ended—Tokyo 21, Hiroshima 14—and Fumiko still hadn't returned, I trudged off to find her. Through the window of the noodle shop, I could see panpan girls eating and yawning and smoking, gathering themselves, I supposed, for what they hoped would be a post-game rush. Bits of gristle and scraps of paper ticked down the street as if borne along by the roar of the crowd. A few days later, I would read an article about the Atom Bowl in *Star & Stripes*. The writer described a private named William Wall coming off the bench and scampering for two long touchdown runs to give Hiroshima the victory, and I would wonder if this was the same Willie Wall I'd met so many months before, the one who'd tried to dance with Namiki but was refused. I like to think so but never did find out for sure. I missed the fourth quarter altogether. Fumiko was sitting on a bench outside the train station, lips pale, teeth chattering, eyes red-rimmed. From that distance, the crowd noise was muffled but persistent, like the steady murmur of rain. This time, when I asked what was the matter, she leaned into my arms and started crying again, talking fast through her sobs, repeating the word *mittomonai, mittomonai, mittomonai,* but I didn't know what that meant so I just held her and told her everything would be all right. Our train was waiting empty at the platform, and I led her on board to get her out of the cold. As soon as we found our seats, Fumiko reached for my zipper. I brushed her hand away but she said, "Thank you very much for this gracious invitation," and she reached for me a second time and I wasn't man enough to make her stop. She hiked up her dress, still crying, and I lowered my fly and pushed her back across the row of seats and sank myself between her legs. It didn't take long. By the time the first few soldiers came trickling back from the game, we were dressed and composed, sitting side by side like nothing at all had happened, neither speaking a word.

Mittomonai translates roughly as indecent or shameful. I looked it up when I got back to the barracks. But I don't think I understood what Fumiko meant, not right away at least, not until some time had passed. At first and for a long while afterward, I thought she meant the idea of such a celebration at the scene of such a tragedy, but now I think her meaning was more complicated than that.

We returned to Tokyo just after midnight, said our goodbyes on the platform. We hadn't spoken for hours. I think we understood that this was not the beginning of something but the end.

The following week, she came around to clean the barracks like nothing had changed, and I was glad. One evening, I returned from the OPS to find Clifford's seppuku sword waiting on my bed, and I knew Fumiko had left it there. A strange alchemy of emotion went surging through me—part sorrow, part guilt, part envy, part gratitude to Fumiko. I began to think that what had happened between us was one of those moments in life that has no explanation whatsoever and would fade into nothing after enough time had passed. Maybe I would remember those few minutes sometimes in the middle of the night, or maybe it would become a story I would tell in some future version of life that I couldn't begin to imagine now, a war story or the nearest I had to such a thing. But it turned out that I was wrong about all that. What happened on the train had an effect I could never have anticipated.

Ten days after the Atom Bowl, I received another letter from my wife.

Well, he's here. Francis Michael Beck. Named for you and for my father. Born December 15, a few minutes after midnight. Every mother believes that her child is the most beautiful in the world, but I'm the only mother who is right. I've enclosed a picture for proof. I was still loopy from the ether when they took him to the nursery, and for the rest of the night I couldn't stop worrying that they would never give him back. I didn't sleep. I kept getting up to watch him through the window in his bassinette. I was afraid someone would spirit him away to punish me for the circumstances of his birth. But in the morning the nurse brought him to my room and laid him in my arms and I knew that, whether I deserved it or not, I was forgiven. This child is mine forever and I am the most grateful girl in the world. Because my son is healthy. Because you have been so kind. Because my own father is holding him as I write and I can see that he's in love. Somehow the world has let me off the hook. I know you can't share my joy in this moment. That would be too much to ask. But please, Van, no matter what happens next, know that I am happy.

It was hard to tell anything about the baby from the picture. He was wrapped in a blanket in my wife's arms and all I could make out was his face, pinched with frown. My wife was propped up in bed. Her eyes looked tired but her hair was brushed and I thought she'd put on some lipstick. She was smiling around a cigar between her teeth, and I remembered that part of what had drawn me to her in the first place, what had made dancing with her at the USO something to look forward to, was her willingness to kid around. It struck me that she was a girl you'd be lucky to fall in love with and I thought, without really thinking it, without being able to put the thought into words, that maybe what had happened with Fumiko had evened things out between us and, whatever awaited in the future, we could proceed as equals now. Of course, this was just a feeling. I wasn't looking down the road. At the time, I was just a soldier sitting on a bench in Hibiya Park admiring a picture of a pretty girl and her child.

My discharge papers came through in February. I suppose I should have been expecting them—most men counted down the days like kids waiting for Christmas—but somehow the news caught me off guard. Captain Embry called me into his office to deliver the standard speech. The army appreciated my service et cetera but there was still work to be done, plenty of opportunities for a cocksucker like me if I would consider sticking around. Not long before, I would have reenlisted in a flash.

Two more weeks would pass before I boarded the troopship to Hawaii, then the plane to San Francisco, and finally the train back to Mobile. I spent my last days in Tokyo like a tourist. Bought a pair of blood-red vases on the Ginza for my mother. Watched Kabuki shows. Visited the shrine of the Amida Buddha, the famous statue there. This Buddha was not fat and jolly like the souvenirs for sale at the PX but young and slim and thoughtful-looking. One night, I attended a performance of *The Mikado* at a theater renamed for Ernie Pyle. A traveling company was in town from the States. I'd never seen operetta before. Operetta wasn't too popular in Alabama. The show was set in Japan, but all the Japanese characters were played by Americans. They did songs about lost love and secret identity. There was a song about beheading. The officers and their wives were howling, but the locals in the audience just blinked and frowned. I didn't get it either. Throughout the show, the box closest to the stage kept its curtains pulled except for a turret-narrow slit. During intermission, I heard a rumor that Emperor Hirohito himself was up there watching, and I felt at once thrilled to be in the presence of real royalty and embarrassed for the man. All that silliness and singing and him a direct descendant of the gods. I bummed a cigarette, though I hardly ever smoked, and walked outside. A rickshaw rolled by on the street, two GIs in back, two old men at the rails. One of the GIs shouted, "Which way to New Orleans?" and I pointed with my cigarette. When the lights flickered, calling everybody to their seats, I returned to the barracks instead.

I tried, during those weeks, not to think about Arthur MacArthur, or I told myself that he was better off left alone, and while that might have been true, I couldn't make myself believe it and I wanted to see him, if not for his sake then for mine. So I steeled myself and rode the elevator up to Bunny's office to request permission to visit Arthur one last time. He kept me waiting for hours but didn't send me away. I watched his aide lead a procession of well-dressed local men in and out, mid-level dignitaries, I guessed, the stream of them broken now and then by some officer on business who was allowed to cut in line. Finally, Bunny's aide informed me that the General could spare a minute, and I found him at his desk massaging the bridge of his nose like his eyes were tired.

"So you're going home?" he said.

"Yessir."

"I envy you. Days like today, I believe I'll be in this office til I die. The Japanese are used to being led. It was the Imperial family for however many thousand years, and then it was the generals, and now it's us. If we pack up, it'll be the Reds, and I won't stand for that."

His office was small and windowless but still imposing. Dark wood and leather. A framed quote from someone named Lucius Aemilius Paulus on the wall:

> If anyone thinks himself qualified to offer advice respecting the war which I am to conduct, he will be furnished with a ship and a tent; even his traveling costs shall be defrayed. But if he thinks this is too much trouble and prefers the repose of the city to the toils of war, let him not, on land, assume the role of pilot.

The chair behind Bunny's desk was the only one in the room, so visitors were forced to remain standing before him.

"I assume," he said, "that you're here because you want to see my son before you go. Bid him a fond farewell and such?"

"Yessir."

"Good," he said. "That's good. I was beginning to worry I'd misjudged your character."

I was prepared to make a case, but that was that. He instructed me to present myself at the residence at 0900 then dismissed me with a wave.

Fog was riding low over the ground when I set out, but it was starting to lift by the time I arrived. Mrs. Bunny had sent Ridges to meet me at the gate. I could see the Packard idling in the drive, exhaust mingling with the last remnants of the fog. We conducted our business through the bars.

"Is Arthur with you?"

Ridges shook his head. "I'll go get him in a minute. But the missus wants to be sure you understand. I'll fetch Arthur and we'll run you to the barracks, but that's it. No stops, no detours. The shortest way there and back."

"That's barely fifteen minutes."

"Take it or leave it," Ridges said. Then he sighed and his voice softened a little. "Look, I don't know what all you done or what's going on and I don't want to know, but I can tell you this is the best you're gonna get. The missus is pretty hot."

"This is strange, isn't it?"

"Well," Ridges said, and he stood there looking at me.

"I'll wait," I said.

I watched him back the car around and roll off toward the residence, my breath coalescing in the cold. The driveway was lined with evergreens, so after a second the Packard disappeared around a bend. I heard the faraway sound of car doors opening and closing, and then the Packard reappeared a minute later and a guard emerged from the guardhouse and Ridges stopped, leaving room for the swinging gate. Ridges nosed the Packard through and the guard shut the gate behind him and I climbed in back. Arthur had one of his cast-iron soldiers in his hands.

"This a one-way trip," Ridges reminded me. "Express."

He shot me a glance in the rearview but I ignored him.

"Who's that you got there?" I said to Arthur.

He held the figure up so I could see him, but didn't speak or look at me. The figure in his hand was Robert E. Lee.

"The greatest military mind in history," I said.

I knew Arthur preferred Hannibal and I hoped to get him caught up in the debate, hoped maybe that would start him talking, but it was clear he'd made up his mind to pout.

"Look, I'm sorry I haven't been to see you in so long. A lot has happened. I can't really explain it all. But I wanted to be here. I really did."

Nothing.

"Talk to me, Arthur. Please. We'll be at the barracks in a minute."

Still no reply. We were coming up on the bombed-out buildings and the baseball diamond. As usual, there was a game in progress, a dozen or so boys in school uniforms knocking the ball around.

"Stop the car," I said and Ridges said, "You must be outta your damn mind."

"I mean it," I said. "You and Arthur can do whatever you want, but I feel like playing ball."

Ridges eyed me in the mirror. To my surprise, he eased the Packard over to the shoulder. I turned to Arthur.

"Bye, buddy. It's been nice knowing you."

I offered my hand but he refused to take it, so I stepped out of the car and headed for the diamond without looking back. I hailed the boys in Japanese. They watched me coming like I was a figment of the imagination, scary but decidedly unreal. I chanced a look over my shoulder. Ridges was in the process of turning the car around but I could see Arthur in the back seat, the shape of him, waving his hands and pointing. I beelined for the pitcher's mound, explained as best I could that the son of General MacArthur was in that car and he would like to join their game—not for long, just a single turn at bat. The pitcher was perfectly still as I spoke, his eyes never leaving my face. I explained that Arthur MacArthur was a few years younger than he was and should be pitched to accordingly and did he, the pitcher, understand? He shifted his gaze to the Packard. They were stopped in the middle of the road but nobody was getting out and I was beginning to worry that my ploy would fail, that Ridges would convince Arthur to obey his mother or, worse, that I didn't mean enough to Arthur to be worth the consequences of disobedience. But after a second, the back door swung open and Arthur made his way sheepishly over the grass, eyes on his shoes, his hands stuffed into the pockets of his corduroys.

"You're up," I said.

It speaks volumes about the nature of Arthur's life that he recognized nothing unusual in the fact that the game was being put on hold for him, the batting order interrupted so he could have a turn. He just shuffled over to the plate, took the bat from the boy who'd been waiting there, and rested it listlessly on his shoulder.

"All right," I said. "Play ball."

Arthur let the first pitch go by despite the fact that it was a perfect strike. The pitcher was doing his best to keep everything slow and easy, but Arthur whiffed the next ball even so. The third, he shanked foul behind the plate. I gave the pitcher a look, patted the air with my hands. Bunny would have been furious but I didn't care. I was more worried that Arthur would strike out. To my great relief, the next pitch came in fat and sluggish and Arthur got around on it, sent the ball looping high and deep and straight into the glove of the kid playing center field. But Arthur didn't notice that he was out. He was already sprinting past first base and closing on second at top speed, arms pumping at his sides, little tufts of dust rising from his heels. The center fielder held the ball and we all watched Arthur take third on the fly and make the triumphant turn toward home.

Back in the car, once again rolling toward the barracks, Arthur fished Robert E. Lee out of his pocket and thrust him into my hands.

"Here," he said.

The figure was barely two inches tall but had more heft than you'd expect. Right hand over his heart, left holding his hat off to the side, below his waist, like he'd removed it in supplication. The detail on his paint job was amazing. Gray uniform with brass buttons. Black leather riding boots. The white of his hair and beard. The kind blue of his eyes. His expression seemed equal parts sadness and surprise and, though Arthur had never specified one way or the other, I'd always imagined that this was Lee at Appomattox or at Gettysburg just after the horror of Pickett's charge.

"I can't keep this," I said.

"But you gave me those samurais," he said. "Plus I have another Lee. The one on horseback."

"What's his horse's name again?"

He answered, "Traveler," without missing a beat, and his certainty made me smile.

"All right. Thank you. I'll take good care of him."

"You were just kidding before, right?" he said. "You know Hannibal is the greatest general of all times?"

"No way," I said. "Lee."

"Hannibal."

"Lee."

Arthur huffed and grimaced. "Hannibal conducted a successful campaign on enemy soil without reinforcements. This is not to mention the Alps. He won every battle with half the army. He would have won the war if the Romans hadn't been afraid to fight fair."

"What about Chancellorsville?" I said.

"Oh, come on," he said, and he would have gone on arguing if I hadn't pulled him up close and knuckled his head.

After they dropped me at the barracks, on the way up to my room, I heard the drizzle and slap of a mop being drawn out of a bucket, the swish of it across the floor, and I knew Fumiko was swabbing the john. She was humming as she worked. I leaned against the wall to eavesdrop and after a few bars, I recognized the song. I don't remember all the Japanese, but in English the lyrics went something like this: *Red apple to my lips / The blue sky is watching / The apple doesn't say a word but the way it feels is clear.* The song didn't make much sense to me, but it had been a hit on local radio the year before. For a couple of months, you heard it everywhere you went. I listened for a minute, Fumiko's humming echoed and amplified by the tile, then ducked past the door and down the hall to start packing my bags.

X

I'm typing all this on a 1955 Royal Quiet Deluxe. I still have the Super Speed, but I keep it in its case on a shelf in the hall closet. My souvenirs from the war: a military issue typewriter and Arthur MacArthur's cast-iron soldier. I presented Clifford's seppuku sword to my father when I got home. He held it in both hands, gave it a good look, thanked me, and then turned on the radio to listen to the news while my mother oohed and ahhed over her vases. I rattled around the house for a week before anybody inquired about my plans. I'm sure they suspected something wasn't right. Would I bring my wife back here, they wanted to know, or would I go to her? I told the truth. I told them everything. We were eating dinner at the time. My mother dropped her fork and covered her mouth with both hands. My father stared into his mashed potatoes while he considered his reply.

"I could probably get you on as bargeman."

I didn't want to be a bargeman and I told him so, but it turned out they were hiring typists, too. The war had pulled everybody out of the Depression. They didn't need more typists, not really, but my uniform plus my father's years of loyal service sealed the deal. For the rest of the spring and through

the summer, I typed invoices and shipping orders and memo-
randums, all of it passing before my eyes and leaving not a trace.
The difference, in this case, was that the haze never quite lifted
from my mind. My father was off on his tugboat most of the
time, and my mother and I had the house to ourselves, but when
he was home, we listened to Alabama play football on the radio
together. Alabama had a new coach that fall, Harold "Red"
Drew, and though his team did one game better than the previous season, they lost three, including the Cotton Bowl, and
we agreed that, all in all, the season was a disappointment. I'm
not sure if these two things are related, but at the beginning of
the new year, with the taste of disappointment still in my mouth,
I decided that the life I had been living since the army was no
life at all. The last of my service pay was still earning interest in
the bank, and because I had no rent to worry about I'd managed to save a fair portion of my salary as a typist. I bought a
ticket on the Crescent Line, which runs from New Orleans,
through Mobile, all the way to Washington, D.C. There I could
switch trains and keep going until I reached New York. If I
liked what I found, I'd look for work. A skilled typist can always make ends meet. If New York didn't suit me, I'd buy
another ticket on another train and ride west on the heels of
countless Americans before me. Such was the extent of my plan.

To pass the time on the train, I read half a dozen different
newspapers and, to my surprise, in all of them I found rum-
blings about Bunny running for President. He hadn't officially

declared his candidacy, but a nominating committee had been formed, whatever that means, and the editorialists seemed enflamed by the idea. In Atlanta, the paper was for a return to isolation, while Bunny represented American meddling in world affairs. In Richmond, he was criticized for not coming down hard enough on the Reds, for allowing the Communist Party to exist in Japan at all. Anyone reading these pages will be aware that he failed to win the Republican Party nomination in 1948 and that, in a few more years, he would be called away from Tokyo to fight the communists in Korea. I did not, of course, know any of that at the time. I exited the train in D.C., intending to see the sights, and as I gazed at the White House through the iron gates, I couldn't help thinking that not only Bunny but Arthur would enjoy life in such a place just fine.

Before I left D.C., I took the street car to Arlington National Cemetery and walked the rows of crosses. Despite the cold, there were plenty of other soldiers out, lots of wives and mothers, too. I had no particular grave to visit, so I drifted among the long interred, trying to keep as far as I could from the real mourners. This wasn't difficult, as the dead were grouped according to the war in which they died, and I spent most of my time among men who gave their lives to preserve the Union. I wondered, as I suppose all men wonder in such a place, if I possessed the courage to march in neat formation into the barrage that awaited those old soldiers. And I wondered if courage or some less respectable synonym was required to order men into that barrage. In the distance, I could see a dark blue canopy casting a shadow over a particular patch of ground. At first I thought it must have been left over from a ceremony the day before, but then I thought the army was too efficient to leave such a thing standing overnight and it must be waiting for a service still to come. I didn't want to hang around for that.

An hour north of D.C., en route to New York, the train paused in Baltimore, and I got off. I hadn't premeditated anything but the dead were much in mind, and I remembered Clifford's address from all those letters. His parents occupied the second floor of a rowhouse on Saint Paul Street, nearly identical to the dozens of other rowhouses on the block. The rooms led one into another, living room first, then a dining room with a coal fire burning in the hearth, then a master bedroom, then the bathroom, and behind the bathroom, tacked on like a closet and not much bigger, was Clifford's room. There was just enough space for a single bed and a bureau. The kitchen ran along the side of the house, narrow as a hallway, and that's where his mother served me coffee. I had introduced myself as a friend of her son and I couldn't tell if she was pleased to have me there or not. She was wearing a housedress and step-ins and she kept looking at me like I was trying to pull a fast one. She poured a splash of Irish whiskey into her coffee but offered none to me.

"So you were Clifford's roommate?"

"Yes, ma'am."

"Whatever happened to that motorcycle?"

Her question caught me off guard and it took a moment to regroup.

"He sold it, I think."

"I thought it belonged to both of you."

"That's right," I said. "It did."

"For how much?"

I blinked and reddened.

"I don't recall exactly. But that's one reason why I'm here." I reached for my wallet. "I found some money after. . . . I thought you should have it." I had forty-seven dollars on me. The rest was in my duffel, tucked away in a locker at the station. I removed two tens and four fives and laid them on the table. A nice round number seemed best, most believable, but she was unsatisfied.

"You came all this way to bring me forty dollars?"

"No, ma'am." I hesitated. The truth was I wasn't sure why I'd come. I didn't know what the army had revealed about the circumstances of his death. "I just wanted to tell you I was his friend. He had a lot of friends."

"Of course he did. My Clifford was always good with people."

"He was a good man."

Her mouth twisted into a sour smile.

"He did a bad thing," she said.

I said, "But—" and then I stopped because I couldn't imagine how to finish the sentence. I didn't want to complicate matters by telling her about Namiki, didn't know if that would make her feel better or worse. I pushed my chair back, thanked her for the coffee.

"Wait," she said.

She disappeared into the back of the house, and I walked into the next room to move myself closer to the door. The heat from the fireplace made it hard to breathe. When she returned, she was carrying a small black box. Inside, pinned onto a background of velvet, was a silver star for valor.

"He sent this home after the surrender," she said. "It's hard to . . ." Her voice trailed off and I thought she was going to cry, but she controlled herself. "Do you have a silver star?"

"No, ma'am," I said. "I wasn't as brave as Clifford."

Two hours later, I was sitting on a bench in the station letting one train, then another, set off for New York without me. The high arched ceiling made echoes of footsteps and squealing brakes and bounced random snippets of conversation back down to the floor, and I had the sense of being poised outside of time, while the world was rushing by at twice its normal speed around me. I was trying to remember the most courageous thing I'd ever done and failing in that moment to think of anything. Just before the clock in the tower struck 2200 hours, I returned to the ticket window and bought a seat on the night's last southbound train. Rode it through Virginia in the dark and the

Carolinas and into Georgia, where I hoped to settle what remained between me and my wife.

My wife was raised in one of those sawmill towns in that part of the South, not quite big enough to be called a city but big enough to have a civil war monument on the courthouse lawn. A river with an Indian name runs along its fringe, and if you float the current downstream a little ways it will carry you to Fort Benning.

I arrived just after noon, downtown quiet at lunch hour. Winter sunlight made watery dapples on the street and on the grass of the courthouse square. I remembered how to find the house, and though it was several miles from the station I decided to walk. I wanted some time to think before I made my presence known. The road was walled with pines, broken occasionally by a red clay track leading back into the woods or by a clear-cut field, but there was nothing growing now. My wife lived with her family in a section of mill housing not far from the river. Her father was a foreman so they had three bedrooms and a parlor, but to get there you had to pass the one-room shacks occupied by the Negroes, then the two- and three-room places where the poor whites lived. The closer you got to the river, the more respectable the neighborhood appeared. All the way, I considered my options. My thoughts kept darting around behind my eyes. I'd been betrayed. That was at the bottom of all this. My wife had given birth to another man's child. But those words rang hollow in my mind, and I couldn't help feeling thrilled at the prospect of seeing her again.

They were finishing lunch when I arrived. The dining room curtains were open. I stood in the yard and watched. Her mother was clearing the dishes and her father was drinking coffee while he read the paper, making an effort, I thought, to ignore my wife nursing her child across the table. A blanket was draped over her chest so I couldn't see the boy but I couldn't take my eyes off her, chin tipped down, hair swept behind her ear. Eventually, she looked up and said something to her father and her gaze fell on the window and she noticed me standing there outside. For a moment, she registered nothing at all. Then she recognized me, and to my surprise what I saw on her face was fear, so thorough and unmistakable I glanced over my shoulder in case something terrible was behind me. When I turned back to the window, she was gone. I assumed she was coming out to greet me but it was her father who appeared on the porch. Arms crossed. Balding.

"What do you want?" he said.

"I'd like to speak to my wife."

He pulled a funny scrunched-up face. It was clear he didn't know how to treat me. I was the man who'd married his daughter without permission but that wasn't so bad as the man who'd gotten her pregnant and left her to raise the child alone. He puffed his cheeks with air, and when he released the breath it was as if he were deflating head to toe.

My wife stepped out of the shadows and touched his arm. "It's all right, Daddy."

Her father looked relieved. "I'll be inside if you need me," he said, and he left her on the porch, and my wife stood there appraising me, getting her bearings, feet apart as if for balance, both hands cupped atop her head.

"Hey," I said, and after a moment, she said, "Hey," and then she waved me inside and introduced me to her son. He was a year old by then, no longer an infant but not quite a little boy. There was no great jolt of affection at our first meeting. I directed the usual compliments to his grandparents and gave the boy a handful of 10-sen coins I'd been carrying around, the ones with the hole in the middle and flowers on both sides, and asked my wife if we might have a minute or two alone.

In a quiet voice, after everyone else had left us, she said, "I'm not scolding, but you can't give change to a baby. He'll put it in his mouth."

"I'm sorry," I said. "I didn't think."

"He'll be fine. Mother's with him."

"I should have brought a better present."

"That's not necessary," she said.

"I should have brought something for you."

"Don't be silly," she said, and so it went.

After half an hour, I asked if it would be all right for me to stick around a few days and she said, "If that's what you want," and I took my leave and hunted up a room in a boarding-house downtown.

Mornings, after her father had left for work, we'd stroll young Francis in the park or sit on the porch swing while he dozed in her arms or played at our feet. Nights, after he was asleep, I would escort her to the movies or dinner or down to the river to watch the stars. This town was small enough that my presence made for good gossip, and I took a kind of plea-sure in the scandal that we caused. We were allied by it, and the pressure of the outside world made me want to assert my-self in opposition. All the while, my wife was lovely and strong and I understood that she was no longer the girl I'd proposed to on a whim. She told me about waking up in the middle of the night sometimes, paralyzed with fear for Francis, and I told her how things had ended for Clifford and Namiki. I didn't tell her that I sometimes wondered if I'd ever be so desperate, so possessed by love. We never spoke of divorce. The subject loomed on the periphery of our time together and I kept wait-ing for it to intrude, but then my wife let me lead her to my bed, and I knew I'd made a promise to her.

"Do you know the Bible?" my wife said.

A curious question, I thought, given she was at that mo-ment sprawled beside me in the dark, her dress and stockings draped over a chair. I remembered those nights typing scrip-ture with my mother. I remembered the day I learned Clifford was dead.

"I guess," I said.

My wife made her voice pious and grave. "*Let not sin reign in your mortal bodies, to make you obey their passions. Do not yield your members to sin as instruments of wickedness but yield yourselves to God* as something something something *and your members as instruments of righteousness*. My mother read that to me while I was on bedrest. Romans, 6:13. I told her she'd missed the boat."

A bubble of laughter was rising from my belly. I tried to hold it down but the laugh came barking out of me and my wife laughed too and rolled toward me and rested her cheek on my chest. Her hair tickled my nose.

"Righteous members," I said, and we laughed again.

My wife said, "We're so wicked," but I didn't feel wicked at all.

Now Tojo is dead and I assume Eguchi is still in prison and I'm ashamed to admit I don't know what's become of Arthur. Of Fumiko. More than two hundred thousand servicemen were stationed in Japan. The vast majority of them, like me, returned alive. A man must be overpoweringly dense, his sense of self girded by ignorance and blindness, to spend so many months in such an alien place and emerge indifferent, but I have the idea nevertheless that very few of my fellow soldiers would point to their time in Japan as particularly profound. They would, if pressed, name wilder days instead, when the world was still aflame, when fate hung still in the balance. Those days in Japan were too peaceful by and large, proof that all those lives were not taken in vain and that what we wanted to believe about the better nature of humanity was true. This impression is not false. I share it on occasion. Even so, what I've been trying to explain for all these pages is how what happened there led me here—to this night in this bright kitchen ticking out these words.

When I was a boy, my mother used to take me down to the docks to watch my father's tugboat pulling out. I remember coins of light reflected on the water and seagulls turning circles in the air. I remember the smell of mud and brine. I remember the sight of my father in the wheelhouse, my mother and me waving until our arms were tired. A decade later, I boarded a ship with a thousand other men and it bore me into the rest of my life. That's not the whole story by a longshot. I know that. The rest of my life was unspooling even as I watched my father's tugboat motor out of sight and it unspools right this minute, while my wife and namesake are sleeping down the hall. But on nights like tonight, when the house is quiet and the moon is full and the world outside this kitchen is a half-remembered dream, it feels like the whole story. I don't know if I have chosen this life or it has chosen me.

One morning, a few days after we moved away from my wife's hometown, she suggested that I take Francis for a picnic in the park. She wanted to finish unpacking, she said, and she couldn't do so properly with the two of us underfoot. In those days, I was uneasy alone with Francis, but how could I refuse? We fed the ducks. We ate the sandwiches my wife had prepared. Francis watched me skip rocks on the pond. I carried him on my shoulders as we walked home. I was a matriculating student at the time, riding Truman's GI Bill, and no one in that new place was aware that he is not my son. About halfway home, we had to stop at an intersection to let a funeral procession pass, a patrol car out in front, the hearse, the mourners with their headlights on, fenders glinting in a way that seemed at odds with the occasion. A negro woman was waiting on the curb, a basket of laundry on her hip. She hardly noticed us, just shook her head and *tisk*ed her tongue as the cars rolled slowly by.

"This a sad world," she said, and I said, "Sometimes," and she turned to see who had replied. Looked us up and down. Smiled, first at Francis, then at me. "He got your eyes," she said.

I blushed and said, "Most people think he looks like his mother," which is how I always respond to that sort of courteous mistake.

Then Francis reached down and covered my eyes with his hands. He was making a little joke, I thought—*he got your eyes*—but it's hard to know for sure with kids. His hands were wrinkly and sweet-smelling, small as paws but big enough to block out the sun.

Acknowledgments

In his prefatory note to *A Quiet American,* Graham Greene wrote, "This is a story, not a piece of history." If I could think of a better way to say it, I would do so here. While *The Typist* does feature several real life historical figures, and while there are plenty of story elements based on actual events, I want to be clear that I have exercised loads of creative license regarding all of the above. This is a work of fiction, plain and simple. I have relied on a number of texts in this endeavor, in particular *Embracing Defeat,* John Dower's remarkable account of the occupation from the Japanese perspective; *American Caesar,* William Manchester's biography of MacArthur; *MacArthur's Japan,* Russell Brines's famous history of the occupation; and *Gaijin Shogun* by David Valley, a former member of MacArthur's Honor Guard. I need also to acknowledge George Garrett's military fiction, collected in *The Old Army Game.* Nobody does the texture of army life like George Garrett. As is the case with most of my work, the final draft turned out quite different from my initial conception, but I should add that I had the first inklings of this story after reading an article headlined, "Football: In 1946, a Search for Relief on a Desolate Nagasaki Field" in *The New York Times* (December 29, 2005). The article sketched

Acknowledgments

the details of an actual football game played by American marines in Nagasaki. Readers will note that I have taken great liberties with this event, including relocating it to Hiroshima. This basic notion germinated until the summer of 2007, when I had the good fortune to meet Richard Waller at the *Writing the Region* conference in Gainesville, Florida. Mr. Waller was a typist in MacArthur's command and not only has he lent my protagonist a profession, he was kind enough to let me pester him about the life of an enlisted man in Tokyo during the occupation.

As usual, I owe an unpayable debt to my agent, Warren Frazier, and my editor, Elisabeth Schmitz and all the early readers of this manuscript—Jim McLaughlin, Murray Dunlap, Jessica Weintraub, B. J. Leggett, Tom Franklin, Beth Anne Fennelly and Shannon Burke. I need to thank Professor Jon LaCure, my colleague at the University of Tennessee, and Charles Schmitz for double-checking my Japanese. Most of all, I need to thank my wife, Jill, and my daughters, Mary and Helen. For everything.

Thank you, thank you, thank you all.

Q&A with Michael Knight

by Kierstyn Lamour

Q: How old were you when you discovered you could tell a story?

A: Let me say first that I feel like I'm still learning and will always be learning how to tell a story. My new novel, *The Typist,* is different from my first novel and I'm sure my next book will be different than this one. I believe that writers need always to be growing and changing, experimenting, taking chances. Otherwise, stagnation can set in. But I've been writing in some form or another since I was a kid. My mother still has "novels" that I wrote in middle school. None of them are more than ten or twelve pages long. The pleasure of it, then and now, is that feeling of getting lost in some other imagined world or of living in someone else's skin. It's thrilling. I've said before that I write fiction because I love to read it.

Q: In your acknowledgments, you wrote that you had the first spark for *The Typist* after reading an article in the *New York Times* about a football game played in 1946 in Nagasaki. Is this a typical way of finding inspiration?

Michael Knight

A: Honestly, no. I'm generally inspired on a much smaller scale—some random image seen from my car as I'm driving down the interstate or an overheard line of dialogue, anything that begs exploration in a story. Newspaper articles are pretty self-contained. They already have a beginning, middle, and an end. The writer has already decided what's most important about the subject. But in this particular case, I stumbled across two topics of real interest to me. I'm a huge college football fan—if memory serves, I ran across the *NYT* piece while Googling for other articles on college football—and both my grandfathers fought in WWII, one in Europe and one in the Pacific, so there's a personal connection there as well. This is not to mention the complexity of the scene suggested by the article, this purely American thing (football), a beautiful thing, if you're a fan, juxtaposed against this setting of horrific devastation. My initial idea was to write a novel about the game itself, the players, and I wrote maybe fifty pages in third person, multiple points of view to that end. But it lacked heart. It was all idea. It was just me using characters to intellectualize instead of inhabiting the characters and letting them tell the story. It wasn't until I settled on the character of Francis Vancleave, until I tried telling the story in first person from his point of view, just this sort of ordinary guy bearing witness tp this incredibly complicated and interesting bit of history, that I was able to write the book.

The football game is still in there. Van is given a pass to go to the game by his C.O. But it's just a piece of the larger story now.

Q: How much research did you have to do for this book?

A: Well, it felt like a fair amount to me but my guess is that a historian would say I didn't do very much at all. I read several books that were particularly useful—*Embracing Defeat* by John Dower, *MacArthur's Japan* by Russell Brines, *American Caesar* by William Manchester and *Gaijin Shogun* by David Valley. And I watched the Ken Burns WWII documentary. Incidentally, my hometown, Mobile, Alabama, is one of the featured cities in that film. Very little of the novel takes place on the homefront but the film helped with context. The same is true of military fiction like Mailer's *The Naked and the Dead* and George Garrett's *The Old Army Game.* While there are no combat scenes or basic training scenes or whatever in *The Typist,* those novels and short stories helped give me a sense of what the characters might have gone through before the occupation, helped inform my understanding of the people I wanted to write about. The imagination is not a purely inventive and creative engine. It's fueled by our experience even if we don't realize it all the time. Because I have no literal memory of the place or time it was necessary for me to build up some kind of base of "experience" to begin imagining. I wanted to do enough research that I could imagine this world but not so much that my imagination would be weighed down by the facts, if that makes sense.

Q: You wrote an essay in the *Harvard Review* in which you argued against writing "what you know" because the writers allegiance ends up going with the "the truth" instead of with the story, usually to detrimental effect. Is that something you had to work around when using historical people and places?

A: I wasn't arguing against writing "what you know" so much as arguing that the old saw is often misunderstood by young writers, that writing only "what you know" can have significant limitations because the literal truth of events often blot out or overshadow a more interesting figurative one and that's sometimes a tricky thing for young writers to get their heads around. But if a writer begins with what he knows and applies that knowledge in some more imaginative context he's more likely to arrive in surprising places. That was pretty much the case here. Van is from Mobile, Alabama. Me, too. Yes, sixty years have passed since WWII, but I don't suppose a young man's desires and fears and so forth have changed all that much. He's a big Alabama football fan. Ditto. He's from a Catholic family. Ditto. His father is a tugboat captain. I worked summers all through high school at a shipyard in Mobile so I have some knowledge and experience of that place and circumstance, have been around people like Van's dad. So I started with that basic core of "knowing" and then put Van into this foreign setting, postwar Japan, a place I've never been and a time I knew almost nothing about and turned my imagination loose. I found that what I imagined was often pretty close to the literal truth but it felt like I was making it up as I went along. To me, that sense of invention, of flying without a net, is the most exciting thing about writing fiction.

If you mean the question more specifically in terms of writing real people like General MacArthur, I don't think my answer would change very much. MacArthur is a fairly major character in the book and I wanted to do him justice as a historical figure. So I read some biographies and stuff. But I also needed his portrayal to be an act of creation. If you're just trying to paint of portrait of a historical figure, the character winds up flat, a talking head. If you want a character to live and breathe, if you want to get under his skin, you have to bring your imagination to bear. One of the ways that I was able to make that happen was by focusing on events that are not part of the historical record, like MacArthur's relationship with his son, Arthur, and his friendship with Van. All of that belongs to me—I made it up—and so in a way the Macarthur in those scenes is a purely fictional character. He's also much more real to me now than the man I read about in those biographies.

Q: General MacArthur is referred to in *The Typist* as Bunny. You have to talk about how he won his nickname.

A: I honestly don't know the truth behind it. I came across a fair number of nicknames for him in my reading—Mac, The Old Man, stuff like that, none of them very interesting— but there was only one reference to him as Bunny. I don't remember where offhand. Wherever it was, the nickname wasn't explained. Which made it perfect. It was comical for a man of such importance but it was sort of affection- ate at the same time and the lack of explanation allowed me to own it in a way. It could be mine. I did write an origin story in an early draft. In my version, MacArthur always sleeps in gray West Point pajamas and a matching night cap and so he looks a little like a rabbit. His wife calls him "Bunny" as a term of endearment and is over- heard by some soldiers. Thus the nickname. But I cut all that. It wasn't important to the story and in the end, the nickname feels more ubiquitous, more true without the explanation.

Q: Early on in *The Typist,* MacArthur asks Van to choose his emotional allegiance between football teams: Alabama or Army. Van, in the face of the highest ranking commander on foreign soil, says, "Roll Tide, sir." I wonder if you could elaborate on what this says about his character.

A: The pat answer to that question is that no self-respecting Alabama fan would ever betray the Crimson Tide no matter who he's talking to. But I guess Van's response also says something about his southerness, a sort of regional pride. I think southerners experience place, for better or worse, more intensely than people from other parts of the country and I think this experience is born, at least for me, of a kind of inferiority complex. I've had a lovely education, am pretty well-traveled and so forth but there's always a minute after I meet someone from New York, say, when I feel like a rube. The rest of the country has looked down on the south for so long, sometimes with good reason, that southerners either want to get the heck out of the south or they figure out of way to love the place they're from. That's one reason we're so good at mythologizing ourselves. The state of Alabama may rank 49 out of 50 in education. We may have one of the lowest per capita incomes in the nation. You name the category. But for the better part of a century our football team has been kicking your football team's rear end.

Q: I'm curious about what happens when you sit down and start typing? When you are plotting a story, are you clear about a point you'd like to get to? Do you allow tangents? Do tangents sometimes end up becoming the story?

A: I guess you could say I'm all tangents. I don't really "plot" stories or novels at all. I usually begin with character instead. My plots, such as they are, tend to grow out of a character's experience, his or her needs and desires. Like I said before, I couldn't really get started on *The Typist* until I knew who it was going to be about. I had no story in mind, per se. Just this young man, Francis Vancleave, and this interesting and complicated time and place. There were, I'll admit, three or four scenes that I had in mind from the beginning, born out of some of my research, and those at least gave me a kind of forward lean into the novel. I knew I wanted Van to be present at the football game. I knew I wanted him to bear witness to some of the war crimes trials. So there was a certain amount of figuring out, okay, what needs to happen to get him to this or that place. But I didn't know when I started out that he was going to befriend General MacArthur's son. I can't tell you how pleasantly surprised I was when it dawned on me that that should happen. Van's relationship with Arthur MacArthur is one of the most meaningful in the book and it came as a complete surprise. And that's another of the great pleasures of writing fiction, that sense of wonder and discovery of one's own story. I've always believed in the notion that if you're not surprised by what you're writing, you're reader isn't likely to be either.

Q: You mention Arthur MacArthur—many of your stories feature children and several of them were written before you became a parent yourself. What's so interesting about child characters and have your own children changed the way you think about or create literary children?

A: I think kids can provide an interesting sounding board for adult characters who are mired in their own selfish concerns, their furtive little interior lives. I also think children are natural judges of character. No matter what adults may think of me, I've always taken a certain amount of pride in the fact that I'm generally liked by children and dogs. As far as my own kids go—I have two daughters, Mary and Helen—I think they've confirmed a lot of what I already believed about kids. Kids are uncorrupted. It makes sense that real tension and therefore good fiction can arise when childish innocence butts up against the mysteries of the adult world. Being a parent has effected my writing on one level in particular, I think: Before my daughters, most of my stories featuring children were focused on the child, centered on the child's observations of the adult world. Now they tend to be focused on adult narrators observing and being influenced by their interaction with kids.

Q: *The Typist* is your second novel. You've also published two collections of short stories and a collection of two novellas. Talk a little about the experience of working in the different genres.

A: I cut my teeth as a writer of short stories. And I still love short stories, both as a writer and a reader. Basically a short story takes a novel's worth of emotional complication and compresses it down into this much smaller space, which can make for a very intense reading experience. In a short story what the writer leaves out is as important as what he puts in. And stories are allowed a kind of air of mystery that I love, especially at the end. Stories generally close on an emotional upturn or downturn but all the loose ends aren't necessarily tied up and that really resonates with me as a reader. It's more like life. It feels more true. I think my experience as a story writer has definitely had an impact on my novels. Most of my favorite novels—*The Great Gatsby, As I Lay Dying,* to name just a couple—are less than three hundred pages long. I think that has less to do with a short attention span than with the intensity of the reading experience. The impact of the story is less diffuse.

And I try to bring that intensity to the page when I'm working on a novel—that sense of an emotion compressed into tight quarters, that air of mystery, that feeling that life is more complicated, more ineffable than the words right here on the page.